The ETCH Anthology 2016

Vocamus Press, Guelph, Ontario

Copyright © 2016 The Guelph Public Library
All rights reserved

ISBN 13: 978-1-928171-35-5 (pbk)
ISBN 13: 978-1-928171-36-2 (ebk)

Vocamus Press
130 Dublin Street, North
Guelph, Ontario, Canada
N1H 4N4

www.vocamus.net

2016

CONTENTS

GRADES 11 - 12

1st PLACE
The Shadow of Being — 3
Jordan Waverman

2nd PLACE
Alex's (Seriously Flawed!) Guide to Depression — 8
Veronika Kosir

3rd PLACE
A New Morning — 13
Megan White

RUNNER UP
Till the Day I Die — 17
Maggie Ryan

RUNNER UP
Flora Sapiens — 21
Julia Hohenadel

RUNNER UP
Of Cogs and Gears — 27
Alexa Jacob

RUNNER UP
Even Now — 31
Pooja Sankar

RUNNER UP
Sunken — 36
Celine N. Persaud

GRADES 9 - 10

1st PLACE
Warzone — 43
Ellen Zhang

2nd PLACE
From Frost Comes Flowers — 49
Crystal Lu

3rd PLACE
Through War We Endure — 54
Lily de Loë

RUNNER UP
Colour Blind — 59
Khloe Henderson

RUNNER UP
Deception — 65
Sarah Demary

RUNNER UP
Pursuit of Love — 70
Sabrina La

RUNNER UP
Dawn — 75
Holly Lavergne

RUNNER UP
Scorched — 80
Morgan Curtis

GRADES 7 - 8

1st PLACE
Titles in Motion   87
Julia Llewellyn

2nd PLACE
Unexplained   92
Aluki Chupik-Hall

3rd PLACE
My Name is Mapiya   96
Maeve Brennagh Mackie

RUNNER UP
Luna   99
Luiza Aguilar

RUNNER UP
Alex Von Valentine   104
Victoria Casey

RUNNER UP
The Vaccine   107
Grace Ma

RUNNER UP
The Truth Behind the Flames   111
Grace Mitchell-Qahawish

RUNNER UP
Change is Constant   117
Emily Fritzley

Preface

The stories in this collection are the winners and runners up from the Guelph Public Library's 2016 Teen Writing Contest. They were judged and arranged in the collection by grade level.

The cover of the collection was made using the winning entry of the Guelph Public Library's 2016 Cover Contest, created by Pooja Sankar, a Grade 11 student at Centennial Collegiate Vocational Institute.

Writerly mentorship was provided by Guelph and area authors – Justin Admiral, Shane Arbuthnott, Avril Borthiry, Lisa Browning, Alison Bruce, James Clarke, David Donaldson, Fred Dawkins, Nick Dinka, Jack Florek, Darcy Hiltz, Bill Hulet, Sheila Koop, Garth Laidlaw, Sean McCabe, Michelle Jay, Laura Lush, Claudette Melanson, Robert Young, Matt Payne, Andrea Perry, Marion Reidel, Ryan Toxeopeus, and Sean Warren.

The stories were judged by Elissa Davidson, Jeremy Luke Hill, and Danielle Joworski. The contest was organized and arranged by Elissa Davidson of the Guelph Public Library. The book's cover and interior were designed by Jeremy Luke Hill of Vocamus Press.

GRADES 11 - 12

1st PLACE

The Shadow of Being

Jordan Waverman

It was a sweltering day in the heat of summer, one of the ones where the ground appears hazy and indistinct, and the heat seems to cling to your skin. I was walking down the street on this day, regretting my decision to take a hike. But I'd had to leave home; inside was worse than out. And so there I was. I squinted. It seemed as if the road was vanishing into the distance. But, as aforementioned, it was one of those hazy days, so I took it for a mirror trick and ignored it.

As I approached, however, I realized that it couldn't be a trick. For if it were, then surely the road would appear as I walked forward. But appear it did not; instead the distance between myself and that swirling mist decreased. I stared at it a little harder, sure I was wrong. But I was not wrong . Eventually, the road vanished, there being a hazy stretch before it disappeared into a yawning black pit.

I looked about, however, and was rather surprised to see that I was the only person to notice that the world seemed to vanish (for, upon closer inspection, I discovered that it was not just the road that vanished, but all of reality entirely). Others just ignored it; and if they should try to walk into it, then they would turn about and head the other way with scarcely a thought.

My curiosity piqued, I walked to the end of the world and was pleasantly surprised to discover that I was not the only person to note the hole. There, upon the verge of reality, sat an old man, his body so folded and wrinkled he was barely noticeable. He appeared to be fishing, his line cast over the periphery into the swirling depths. He was wearing a cloak that looked like it had been made in the Sixteenth Century, so faded was it. He looked up at my approach, then shrugged, as if accepting my existence as being some arbitrary factor which could not concern him. Staying well back from the edge so as to avoid falling in (for I feared leaving existence, if that was what this was), I gently cleared my throat to get his attention.

He ignored me, instead reeling in and recasting his line. He appeared to get excited for a moment, as if he'd caught something (though what he was trying to catch was beyond me; I was too far back to see over the cliff), then looked disappointed. He adjusted himself to get more comfortable. Once more, I cleared my throat. This time he glanced over, staring at me with unfocused, cataract-filled eyes. He grunted noncommittally and returned to his task.

"Excuse me…" I began, but he interrupted.

"Not leaving, are we? Figures, you can't take a hint. They never can."

"They…?" I started, but he didn't take the bait, and instead returned to his fishing. We stood there for a few moments, until he heaved out a great sigh. He motioned me over. Hesitant, but filled with an intrepid curiosity, I stepped forward.

"What do you see down there?" he asked, pointing off the edge.

I stepped forwards still more, and glanced down carefully. At first, there was nothing, just an inky blackness such as one only hears about in stories. But on closer inspection, I was shocked to see that objects even blacker than the darkest of pits (which this was), were stirring about down there.

I shivered. "What are those… those… creatures?" I asked breathlessly (I assumed them to be creatures, for they possessed a strange, desperate pattern to their movements that I would not have expected from something such as a cloud, or group of insects).

At first, the man did not respond, and I feared his interaction with me had ceased. But then he seemed to gather the energy to respond, and replied: "Those who never were."

I must confess, I didn't understand. After all, who would? "Those who never were" is not the greatest of explanations. And so I asked him to clarify his statement.

Once more he paused. He was clearly a man who chose his words with an exaggerated care, and I became aware that this conversation could take far longer than I desired. But he eventually responded. "They are the remains of those who never were; the unborn, as you might better understand it. They are the people who, for some reason, never entered this world, though they were meant to. And so their souls are stuck on the edge of the world, meant to be in it but incapable of actually entering, a shadow of the being they were meant to be."

Once he had clarified his statement, I finally understood. My earlier intuitions were correct; I had truly reached the end of reality, and had seen the damned souls who inhabited it. Now that I had been informed, I was able to look closer and perceive the truth. The vague shapes inhabiting those depths possessed a definitively human shape, their features twisted into a horrified grimace. Revolted, I stepped back.

I turned to regard the man, who was watching me closely. "But... why?" I was barely able to stutter it out, so disgusted was I by the fate of those below.

The man merely cocked his head, as if expecting an explanation but not willing to ask for one.

That, I was happy to provide. "Why are they there? How come they are stuck there? And why, all of a sudden, are they visible?"

This time, the pause was veritably painful, as I waited for an explanation. I was surprised by his response, for this man, who in the few minutes I'd known him had seemed to possess such self-assurance, was suddenly indeterminate. "I… do not know," he confided in embarrassment. "There is no explanation as to why they exist, other than fate, I suppose. I believe them to be capable of leaving for a limited amount of time, though they cannot travel far, and are exceedingly weak. When this happens, the edge of reality blurs and becomes visible to a few, such as yourself, until they return. I believe the capacity to view them is linked to severe emotional distress."

I considered this, recalling the bad news from the hospital that had resulted in my leaving the house, trying to collect my thoughts and act with some small degree of wisdom. "So… if they can't travel far, then where is the person who has left? If you and I are here, where is he? Do these people possess names?"

The man stared at me, and for the first time I saw him smile. It was a slim one, sad, and seemed to contain the same odd desperation within it that the beings contained as they moved about. He motioned me closer. Now, for some incomprehensible reason, trusting him completely, I stepped forward. He kept motioning me forward, till I was almost upon him. I could smell his stale breath, see every wrinkle in detail. He motioned me to turn my ear towards him. He whispered but a few words into it. "Corban… That's my name…"

Confused, I looked up, but he was gone, having jumped off the edge of reality. Gone also was the edge, reality having returned to its consistent self. I wondered where it and he had gone, before it occurred to me with an inevitable clarity. I shivered, as if a cold breeze (or a ghost) had blown through me, though I was soaked in sweat in the hot summer day. I turned around then, and headed straight home, thankful yet oddly terrified. As I went, however, my memory of that strange encounter vanished slowly, to my own bewilderment.

By the time I arrived at my door, all memory of the incident was gone, and I sat down on the inside of my door encumbered with a sense of confusion. I was filled with uncertainty, over what I may have seen yet couldn't remember, and a sense that somehow, someway, my reality had been overturned. Yet I couldn't remember… couldn't remember my encounter with that shadow of being.

2nd PLACE

Alex's (Seriously Flawed!) Guide to Depression

Veronika Kosir

I feel like crap. I feel so out of control. I can't stop sleeping. I can't stop eating. A packet of cookies, bags of chips, a hoard of candy wrappers and half-eaten chocolate bars are strewn across the floor. I feel angry, sad, stressed, numb. It's like my feelings are overloading my brain and now there's an emotional power outage in my head.

Sluggishly, my brain reminds me that I have a calculus test tomorrow. My mind screams at my pathetic self to get up and study. My body stays slumped on the sofa. I don't really know how to deal with that. Instead, I decide to consume my body mass in ice cream, sweet, creamy, rich chocolate ice cream…

I have depression. It's hard to admit in person. Since the world has been more open to mental health discussions as of late, I could write a self-help guide based off my personal experience, perhaps, *Alex's (Seriously Flawed!) Guide to Dealing with Depression.*

The first step is recognizing that you have a problem. Signs of depression include: not eating, not sleeping, overeating, oversleeping, neglecting personal hygiene and responsibilities, feeling withdrawn and antisocial, feeling tired, and feeling numb. As soon as you recognize that you have a problem, you should repress all your worries immediately! Convince yourself that you *just need to sleep it off, or that you're just having a bad day… or week… or month…*

After gorging, I decide to go for a walk. The walk is nice, I suppose. The September air is crisp and cool, but pleasant. The sun is setting, painting the sky in bright pink and yellow, soft orange and lilac hues. The trees are a vibrant mix of yellow, red, and green. I don't care.

After that, you need to let your emotions and negativity climb higher and higher. Sometimes, you can try to relieve some of the negativity by writing your feelings in a journal, talking a walk, doing yoga, or another type of outlet. To be brutally honest, this doesn't help much.

Numbness as an emotion is very similar to physical numbness. When your hands get numb because it's too cold, you can't feel your hands, and yet they hurt, much more than when you could feel the cold hitting your skin. It's similar to how I feel as I look at the gorgeous autumn scenery before me. Seeing that the walk isn't helping, I head back. I almost make it to my house before I collapse.

The final step is to let everything build to a crescendo and then let it all gush out like the bursting of a water dam. I highly recommend my favourite method: crying. Ideally, cry in the comfort of your own home, but if you get the urge to cry, you shouldn't repress it. (You probably won't be able to anyhow, but you'll feel more in control if you choose to). My personal favourite places to cry include the school hallways, underneath the sinks in the girl's bathroom, my grandma's bathroom (at two in the morning!). *Once you've left your pillow stained with tears, your eyes puffy and red, and your nose runny, you will feel a lot better (or at least start to feel much better, sometimes it takes a few days).*

Grass, fresh scented and richly coloured, presses against my face, digging into my skin and leaving angry red streaks across my face. The moisture of the earth dampens my clothes and covers my knees and elbows in wet dirt. I return some of the moisture as tears spill down my face back into the ground. I'm crying uncontrollably – on the boulevard of my neighbourhood no less. How embarrassing.

"Are you okay?" a voice asks from above me.

I'm miserable, I think. I hoped no one would approach me in this state, an unknown, sobbing, black-clad human lump, curled up in a rather unusual and regrettably public location.

"I'm fine," I sob, clearly in the middle of being a twenty-four hour flight away from Fine (population: not me, obviously).

"You don't look fine. Is anything wrong?"

"No." Not really. Just my brain.

I look up to see who cared enough to talk to the weird kid lying in the dirt. It's two of my neighbours, one around twenty and the other middle aged, both with dark hair and olive complexions. I've never spoken to either before.

"Hey, she's got her head up. We're getting somewhere!" the older one jokes.

After asking if I was okay and getting a truthful response, they ask me what age I am. "Seventeen," I sniffle. The older of the two nods knowingly.

"Ah. That explains it," he says, with a smile in his voice. "I have three teenaged sons, and they have their emotional troubles too, though they deal with them a little differently." The younger one nods.

"Hey, just try to think about the good stuff in your life! I'm sure you've got something that makes you happy," the younger one says.

"Yeah, I guess I do," I mumble, and it's true. Whenever I have an episode like this, I try to remind myself of my accomplishments and people who care about me. I think of my best friend, and the time he told off my school's version of Donald Trump for calling my arms fat. I conjure up images of my younger brothers, the candy they give me and the time we spend destroying each other at Mario Kart. But the images dissipate and I'm back to feeling empty.

One of the benefits of crying in really weird (and public) places is that you meet people who will restore your faith in humanity. When I cried in the school halls, a girl I barely knew at the time gave me a hug and sat down and chatted with me until I felt better while my best friend fed me chocolate chip cookies. After this stage, you can say, "Adios, depressive episode! Until we meet again!" Unfortunately, you will likely meet again.

"So are your parents at home? How come you're out here by yourself?" the older one asks me.

I sigh. "My parents left for a dinner party, and I forgot my keys in the house," I say, internally cursing my bird-brained tendencies.

"Maybe you could call them?" the younger one suggests. I shake my head.

"Nope, my phone died. Yeah, I've got my life so together right now," I laugh.

"Actually, I'm just heading out right now," the younger one says. "I could give you a ride."

* * * * *

I go to my blog to see seven new messages in my inbox. Excitedly, I go to read them, but people have just dumped a bunch of ignorant comments into my inbox. Oh well, it happens. It's the internet.

How do you even know you really have depression? It's not like you've seen a psychologist to diagnose you.

You're right. I haven't the slightest idea. Similarly, there's no way for me to know I've broken my leg until I see a doctor.

You're just lazy.

You didn't bother to educate yourself before opening your nasty gob. I'm pretty sure that makes you the lazy one here.

I feel sad sometimes too! It can't be that bad!

Consider the following statement: "I feel happy sometimes too! You can't be feeling that great!" That's exactly how you sound, but even more insensitive.

You're depressed because you don't pray to God enough.

Oh, that's funny. That attitude sure reminds me of the attitude people had back in Jesus' time towards people with physical disabilities. I also specifically remember Jesus not approving of that kind of attitude. I'm not saying you're a bad Catholic ("Let him who is without sin cast the first stone," and all), but for heaven's sake! Have you even read the Bible?

It's all in your head!

Golly gee, and all this time I thought it was in my toenails.

You're just doing this for attention. Depression isn't real. It's something millennials made up.

When confronted with someone like this, you should probably just walk away, because arguing with him or her is like playing chess with a pigeon – no matter how skilled your strategy, the pigeon will just knock over all the pieces, crap on the board, and then strut around acting like it won the game. Also, the pigeon doesn't have the brain capacity to play chess. So I delete the message and block the user.

* * * * *

I get out of the car and step onto the soft grass before my parents' friend's home. The scent of barbeque fills the air. My stomach growls, and I remember I haven't eaten dinner yet. I turn around.

"Thank you so much," I say emphatically.

"Oh, don't worry about it," my neighbour reassures me. "You going to be okay?"

I grin. "Yeah," I say. I look up and notice the glimmering canopy of stars above us. "I think I'll be just fine."

3rd PLACE

A New Morning

Megan White

I've been sitting on this ledge all night, waiting for morning. The hard rock beneath me feels wet and cold, and its sharp edges cut into the underside of my thighs. But I don't mind. My feet dangle in the empty air, hovering above the cool clean surface of the water. I extend one bare foot slightly so the tip of my toe prods the surface, creating a single ripple and sending a shiver up my leg. I breathe in the crisp morning air and it cleanses my lungs.

    I've been staring at the reflection of the stars like fireflies on the surface of the dark water. The occasional ripple causes them to sparkle with life. It fascinates me. I've been told that to float in water is to feel weightless as if in space. Staring directly down into the depths of the lake, I see exactly what they warned would be there: darkness, emptiness, and endless possibility. In it I can see myself floating, basking, exploring depths no one has before. I can feel tension building in my muscles: just jump they say. Just jump. But my hands clench the edge of the rock and I hold myself still.

    I continue to stare as the water changes from a deep blue to a warm amber with the rising sun. I finally look up. The lake's surface, as smooth as glass, provides a perfect reflection of the leafless skeletal trees around its edges, the pointed shoulders of rock on which they stand, and the sky lighting up with the dawn above. The sun hasn't yet broken the surface of the horizon. It's almost taunting me, I think, a warm scene as captivating as this. It would be winter soon, the water too cold to touch.

I look down and see that, unknowingly, my foot has slipped into the water. My ankle is submerged. I quickly withdraw it and hug both of my legs to my chest, burying my face in my thighs. What was I thinking? My lip begins to quiver – I didn't realize how easy it was. It was true what they said – the harmonious dance of the waves was entrancing, dragging even the most alert of men in.

I need to come back to reality. I gaze over at the sand shore beside the rock on which I sit. It's not an entire beach, but rather a small alcove that hides in the trees of a dense forest. This is our place: a calm little spot, but the closest thing my family ever had to adventure. A sudden breeze raises a tornado of dancing sand. In it I see shadows of familiar figures. Looking at the beach now, I see my entire past: the dunes in which I used to run; the holes which I would dig for no reason at all; the shade of the trees along the edges where my mother would pile food into our mouths; a large patch of tall grass where I'd lie and gaze at the passing clouds, wondering what my future would hold.

But I also recall the shadow of my mother blocking the warm sun from hitting my face as she loomed over me, her deep grey eyes glossed with concern. She could see in my eyes my thoughts drifting into a fantastic world of the unknown, glorifying the mysterious. It was when she saw this that we would immediately leave the beach. I never blamed her for this though: she often tells me a story of how she had known a little boy my age who also found the dance of the waves captivating. He, the first and last boy to submerge his hand beneath the cool water's surface, found his body leaned so far over the edge of the shore's rocks that he fell. He floated in shock, unable to react before the snakey seaweed hidden from sight beneath the elegant waves wrapped itself around his tiny ankle. His empty chair now sits on the front of his family's porch, reminding me of why daydreaming is dangerous. I see this boy now, sitting as a mirror image of myself on the opposite side of the lake.

I rise from my rock and stride over to the beach. I let my feet sink into its plush warm sand. It stains my wet toes. I don't mind. It's familiar. I could walk this beach blindfolded. The ground supports my feet and the wind hugs me on all sides. I am entirely safe.

I sit myself in the sand, burying my feet in the ground in front of me. Beneath the surface, the dirt is cold and hard. There's a lot less fine sand than there used to be. Hundreds of rainstorms and dozens of floods of the nearby river have eroded the shore so only a skin of dirt remains above the thick layers of cold rock. But I'm safe. The lake sits in front of me, ominous and unforgiving. Here I'm protected, and everything is familiar. What more could I want?

But when I finally get comfortable and somewhat warm, a cold breeze runs its fingers through my hair. Winter is coming – that means the water will soon be too cold to even dip my toe into. Even that would be dangerous.

No. How could I even think it? I'd be punished. Severely. I have no idea what truly lies beneath the surface, and I'm not foolish enough to find out.

But it's as if with this wind I'm reminded of the truth about the shore that I've always felt but never expressed. The sand buries my feet like cement that prevents me from standing. The roots buried in the sand below reach up to me, forming shackles around my wrists. The distant shadows of memory shade me from the light reflecting off the water. The sand used to keep me warm. Now it, like the water, grows cold.

I stare at the silky water. There are miniature waves now, reaching with long arms and clawing with wide hands at the shoreline towards me.

A New Morning

It will be winter soon.

I jump to my feet. I run from the beach. I run from my rock. I run from the shadows and echoes and memory.

I don't stop. I hop from sand to rock. I leap off the edge. I fly. The weight of worry and regret flies off my shoulders. It stays on the shore.

I slice through the surface and my entire body submerges. My arms float weightless on either side of me. My hair leaves my shoulders and floats above my head. My muscles relax. I move slightly with the current. With no wind grass or trees, I hear nothing. Not an echo, not a voice, not a warning.

I open my eyes and the water stings at them. It's wonderful. A world entirely my own. I can discover, explore, adventure. I am myself. I feel safe once again.

I look up. A beacon of light twinkles through the water to my eye. I guess it's morning now.

RUNNER UP
Till the Day I Die
Maggie Ryan

Max disappeared four nights ago. His mother looks as if she hasn't slept in two years and perhaps she hasn't, with three small children, a non-existent husband and now police officers knocking on the door at all hours of the day.

I'm standing at the edge of his family's lawn, contemplating whether or not I should go up, knock on the door, offer my help. The kids like me. Max and I have been friends for years.

I hear footsteps behind me. I turn. It's one of the officers. He's not smiling, although I don't think I've ever seen one smile in my lifetime. He looks kinder than the others as he comes closer, younger, with a softer face, but he too lacks sleep. It occurs to me that I may look the same. Despite his apparent friendliness my stomach drops when I see him. I don't want to talk to him, to be asked the same questions as I was at least five times before.

"When did you last see Max?"
"At school, third period."
"Did he seem anxious or unhappy?"
"He's always anxious."
"Why?"
"A lot of reasons."
"Was there anyone he was afraid of, anyone who was unhappy with him?"
"Of course."
"Who?"

"A lot of people."
"Was he involved with drugs? Are there troubles at home?"
"Yes."

I think they've gotten tired of asking me questions. I'm not trying to hide anything from them. The truth is, I don't know the answers myself. Max didn't like to talk about himself. In fact, he rarely spoke at all, which lead to him being labelled as 'weird' or 'freakish' or not being noticed at all. I know they think it's suicide or that he's disappeared on purpose. I have to admit, I wouldn't be surprised.

"Hey there, you're Max's friend, right?"

Something inside me cringes at his words.

"Yeah."

"I was about to go in and ask, but maybe you can identify this for me?"

He holds out something in his hand, something I hadn't noticed before. It's a hat. A black toque, with a logo of the local brewery on it. I do recognize it. I recognize it instantly.

"Do you know if this belonged to him?"

I stare at the hat. I recognize it because he stole it from me. He almost never took it off, his uncut hair always curling around the edges of it.

Why would he take it off? I take it from the officer. It's heavy and damp in my hand.

"Where did you find it?"

"Bank of the river. Do you recognize it?"

I don't take my eyes off the hat in my hands. "Yeah," I say. "It's mine."

"It's yours?"

"Yes."

"Are you sure? Why was it on the bank?"

"I have no idea."

I turn away from the officer the hat still in my hands. He looks slightly annoyed.

"Thanks for finding it."

* * * * *

I remember the day Max took the hat from me. I have no idea how it came to be in my house, but I was wearing it and we were sitting in my living room. I was painting my nails. I was painting them black.

"Why do you always choose black nail polish?" Max asked.

He was sitting in the love seat across me, watching.

"I like it."

"You look goth. Especially with that hat." I look up at him. "Do not."

"Do too."

"You wear it then." I whipped the hat off my head with my unpainted hand, strands of my hair cling to it, following it as I tossed it across the room to him.

"Fine." He jammed it down on his head. His shaggy hair bounced and curled around the hat. He looked at me. There was a question in his eyes but he didn't say it.

"You look fine," I said, but I wasn't looking at him.

He looked down at his hands. "Will you paint mine too?" His eyes looked the other way.

"So you don't want me to look goth, but you do?"

"No, I want this colour." He held out a pale blue.

I look at him and then at the polish. It didn't go with the hat and he knew it. But I didn't comment on this, instead I just said, "Okay."

His eyes didn't leave his nails as I painted them, and once they were done and dried he leaned back, pushing the hat farther down on his head.

"I won't take this hat off till the day I die."

He seemed more comfortable with the hat almost covering his eyes. His body relaxed. He leaned back into the couch.

"Sure Max," I said.

When I saw him at school the next day, the nail polish was gone, but the hat was still there.

* * * * *

I approach Max's house and let myself in. The television is playing for the kids in the front room, but otherwise the house is quiet. I half expect Max to come thumping down the stairs.

"Mrs. Shannon?"

I walk a little farther into the house. Down the hall to the kitchen.

Mrs. Shannon is standing there, a phone to her ear. Her face is oddly blank and she has the appearance of having been crushed by a thousand bricks.

"Sorry –" I start to turn around, but a choking sound coming from Mrs. Shannon stops me.

"They're –" She can't get the words out. Her voice is somewhere between a whisper and a sob. "They're dragging the river."

"What?"

"They think he's in – in the river."

I can't speak. I don't move. My mind shuts off entirely. The wet hat drips in my hand.

RUNNER UP

Flora Sapiens

Julia Hohenadel

21:00, 07.05.2050

"I guess I should start by apologizing. If you survived, if humanity survived… if you're able to watch this, I guess we didn't totally screw everything over."

I pause, averting my gaze from the camera. This is more difficult than I anticipated.

"For you to understand, you have to realize why we did this. You have to understand our desperation."

"The year is 2050, and the Earth is swollen, saturated with more humans than it can sustain. Earth is plagued with shortages of land to farm, land to live on, water, resources, and especially food. Most nations are succumbing to the chaos and primitive animosity that dwells within the hearts of all humans. All humans jeopardize the survival of their brethren; even the dead pose a threat, as the mass of corpses created each day need to somehow be removed. There's nowhere to bury them, and cremation would mean spewing more greenhouse gases into the air which is already a toxic cocktail of gases. With 10 billion humans to somehow sustain, nothing on Earth is a simple matter."

I pause again. How do I summarize this? How do I compress it so that my entire apology, my plea for forgiveness, can be recounted in entirety before the camera battery dies… or worse?

"Once, before governments were overwhelmed with the impossible task of controlling their people, my team was given a grant. Our mission was to fix something, anything just do what we could to delay humanity's inevitable demise. It was like being given a water gun and being asked to put out a forest fire."

"As is the tendency with young scientists, we were callow and arrogant, our heads were filled with ideas of grandeur. We didn't anticipate the roadblocks, or the funds drying up, or the fact that people would abandon science altogether… Yet despite all this, we still managed to make a discovery."

I pause the film again, rewind. I look so pale in the gloomy light, my eyes beady and bloodshot. The guilt, the terror I feel inside, combined with the screams of the people whose deaths I'm responsible for… I don't get much sleep anymore.

Back on track, I remind myself. Explain. Apologize.

The instant my finger hovers over the play button, the low battery warning flashes. I sigh, shut off the machine, and retire for the evening.

22:37, 08.05.2050

"Sorry it took me so long to get back to you… Today was very busy, what with final preparations and such. Needed to tie up all the loose ends. I'll explain later, but for now, let's continue where we left off last night."

"The main issues which we focused on were food supply and carbon emissions. After years of dead end research, we had nearly given up hope. Then one day my colleague told us of a peculiar sea creature: the green sea slug, an animal which can perform photosynthesis. If sea slugs can do this, creatures not born to photosynthesize, why couldn't we modify humans to do the same?"

"After many trials, and many errors, we were able to insert chloroplasts – and the DNA to operate them – into a human.

Eureka, it worked! While they still need a supplementary form of sustenance, these humans could perform photosynthesis and use the sun to power themselves."

I think back on that day, on the joy, the hope. Maybe if the Earth wasn't so broken we would've waited longer, performed more tests. Maybe we could have prevented this. If only we hadn't been so brazen, so desperate…

"After making our success known, hoards of people began clamouring to become Flora Sapiens, as it was coined. Old people, young people, they all came, and we converted them all. When our country's food consumption per capita plummeted, other countries began to take notice and demanded the same for their citizens. We were known the world over. It was like we were Noah, and everyone wanted on our ark. We obliged.

"We just wanted to save humanity, to solve as many problems as we could. Our goals were pure, you have to understand. Carbon emission? Check; plants turn carbon into oxygen. Food shortages? Solved, Flora Sapiens produce their own food. It was perfect, until it wasn't."

How do I admit to something like this? How to explain that the cold blooded killings are conscious, purposeful, and that I'm responsible.

"As you might have heard, the plant people began attacking humans, regular humans, and eating them." A tear rolls down my cheek. "We should've performed more tests, waited longer before we revealed our discovery to the public. Maybe if we had, we would've known that the photosynthesis would warp their minds and activate a dormant gene which makes them crave human flesh."

"At first, they targeted corpses, like scavengers. A major problem in our world is how to dispose of the dead, so we turned a blind eye. I'm sorry. I'm so sorry." My next sentence is almost cut off by a sob. "We didn't think they'd develop a taste for fresh meat."

I pause again, to collect myself and allow whoever may be watching a moment to fully understand the weight of my words.

"I never thought I'd dread the day the population started plummeting. These plant people are voracious, and humans are, well… plentiful. We only converted about a third of the population into Flora Sapiens.

"I truly apologize for my hand in this bloodshed, in this chaos. But my real confession is this: I'm about to make things worse.

"The Flora Sapiens are going to kill us all. They're in every city in every country, and they look exactly like regular people, so long as they mask their green-tinted skin. You can't trust anyone – not your neighbour, your friends, your family, no one. People are dying, and it's not just because they're being slaughtered like cattle; neighbours are killing neighbours, friends are killing friends, all in the mad belief that those are the people to fear. But we're humans! We don't go down without a fight. Look at us!" I'm shouting now. "There's ten billion people on a planet that can only support half that number! Were survivors, damn it!

"We can't let the Flora Sapiens drive us to extinction. I won't have it; I can't have my failure spell the end of humanity. We are human, and we will go out on our own terms.

"Impact winter. That's the solution! Create a big enough collision and you'll force winter upon the globe. How can the plants survive if they don't have the sun? We programmed them to crave sunlight. Without it they'll go insane, shrivel up, and hopefully die. It will be a literal cold war.

"I did some math, some physics, some hacking. I calculated if we take the abandoned International Space Station and send it crashing to Earth, in just the right place, enough dust and debris will be launched into the atmosphere to blot out the sun – at least for a little while. Just long enough to incapacitate the plant people, give humanity a chance to fight back."

I sigh. "I don't want to do this, but I must. It's the only way to fix this. I have to right my wrong. The Flora Sapiens will die, and humanity might too… but at least the Flora Sapiens will go first."

I type in a line of code which will send the ISS crashing to Earth, and press enter. "Let's watch."

00:00, 09.05.2050

I make my way out of the lab and watch the station as it streaks through the sky. I imagine the people, and the plant people, who gaze upon this now, a meteor gone wrong, a falling star. I struggle to suppress my guilt, my sorrow, and remind myself that this was the only option.

It takes fifteen minutes for the International Space Station to fall. I imagine its descent in three stages. Stage one, where people admire the unexpected light show. Stage two, where they realize it's coming towards them. And finally, stage three, when they realize there's no stopping it.

And then impact. I know fires will spring up, hungrily razing cities, and that the planet will be swallowed by darkness.

But I won't be experiencing any of it.

"I've one last apology to make before I'm done. I'm sorry for what I'm about to do, because I won't be around to see this through. My entire career has revolved around selflessness, to fix the Earth. But right now, I'm going to be selfish."

I reach into my pocket, and pull out a small pill. Potassium Cyanide. I whipped it up in the lab this morning.

"I can't handle my guilt, the fact I created the Flora Sapiens. I can't live with myself after I brought the world to a crashing halt. I hope these videos survive, and someone survives to watch them." I feel a tear roll down my cheek.

Flora Sapiens

"I know I don't deserve it, but I hope I can be forgiven for what I caused. I just wanted to help."

I swallow the pill and sink to the ground, while in the distance the space station collides with the Earth.

RUNNER UP

Of Cogs and Gears

Alexa Jacob

It's been a long time
since they brought me home,
Where I taught her things
she'd never known.

Now I sit hidden
from out of her sight,
And wait for things
to be put right.

I have long since stopped ticking,
My hands frozen in time,
Slowly forgetting
What it felt like to chime.

For years I sat,
in a halo of light.
Watching her learn;
In her line of sight.

She learned to tell time,
And she learned to read,
She waited, she watched,
Until she had to leave.

Of Cogs and Gears

Because clocks, we grow old,
but we never can age.
We may tell the time,
But we can't turn the page.

So for now I just sit here,
Picking up dust.
My cogs and my gears,
Beginning to rust.

    I still remember the day they brought it home. That ticking monstrosity that, like everything else back then, dwarfed me in comparison. The day before, my parents had made the long trek out to the house of my great grandmother to get their fair share as the rest of my large family fought over who got what before the house was sold. As we lived so far away, my mother had been left with the scraps that had either been looked over or were simply unwanted. Still, she had returned victorious with a box of Christmas dishes, three beautiful old vases, an assortment of tea cups and saucers, and a clock so massive and ancient that is was a miracle it survived the long trip down bumpy country roads. I was lucky, too, as, unbeknownst to me, the beautiful chimes would end up singing out the quiet little moments that shaped my life. The quiet ticking didn't just tell time, it told the story of my childhood.

    That night, we all learned why no one else had wanted this grandfather of clocks. The quiet ticking was virtually inaudible in my bedroom three floors up, but I didn't manage more than an hour of sleep at a time thanks to the clock's earth shattering chime, every hour on the hour. After a few days, I became used to the sound, until my parents moved it upstairs and the sleepless night recommenced. The few short days it took to adapt to it felt like an eternity.

Concealed in its shade, I grew to love it. On days when we were expecting company it became the bringer of friends. It was then that I learned to tell time, perched on the arm of the old armchair in my parents' room. I sat, brimming with excitement, with one eye on the slowly spinning minute hand and the other on the street below, should the expected headlights turn into our driveway ahead of schedule.

Ensconced in its shadow was also where I learned to read on my own. On wintery days I would curl up in that chair with my favourite picture book and a mug of hot chocolate. The hands on the clock continued their march around the old face as I attempted to sound out words and often resorted to just looking at the vibrant pictures.

As time passed, however, its use began to dwindle. No matter how fast they tick, even clocks can fall victim to the sands of time. As it looked on, its many relatives were replaced with newer, digital versions. When I started school, I no longer spent my afternoons playing in its shadow. Life grew busier, faster, and the rhythmic ticking could not keep up. The taller I grew, the shorter it seemed; the older I got, the less useful it became. Maybe I was growing up too fast, maybe it was ticking too slowly. Either way, as my life flew by, it was left in the dust.

Crouched in its shroud, I was a child. Out in the light, however, I began to mature. I no longer needed to stare hopefully down the street as I was always notified by a text message when friends were mere minutes away. I no longer noticed when the minute hand began to lag, demanding to be rewound. Nor did I spend lazy Sunday afternoons reading in its shadow; I had my own chair and my own clock in my own room. I no longer wiped off the glass in disbelief when it told me that, yes, I had been sitting there for three consecutive hours. Eventually, I stopped noticing it altogether, it was merely a shape in my parents' sitting room, alone, forgotten, and collecting dust. The slowly dimming chime was so commonplace a sound that even it received little recognition.

As soon as it broke, however, everything changed. It became harder to sleep at night without the consistent ticking. The empty space that marked its former resting place felt wrong, awkward. The fireplace and chair felt lonely. After it happened, I sat for a long time in front of the lines of stain it had left on the wall, realising that it hadn't only worn dents into the carpet, it had also left its mark in me. In its own way, its echoing sound had been both teacher and friend as I made my way down the difficult yet enchanting path that is childhood.

RUNNER UP

Even Now

Pooja Sankar

I seem to be late to class everyday now. This week wasn't any better than the last and high school has almost come to an end just like grade school once did. I'm just not sure which is going to hurt more. It's never easy to give up the past. The present keeps you moving while the past holds you back.

"You have to be kidding, three whole years?" Margaret muttered under her breath.

"Yes, three whole years," I repeated back.

"What's the name, Paige?" Margaret questioned.

"Blake."

I felt myself shudder slightly as I uttered his name. It was a name I had tried to forget for the past four years of high school.

As prom neared, I felt more afraid and stupid all the same. This was not because the concept of prom frightened me, but because a small part of me kept saying, "He will come for you." The bigger part of me just laughed hysterically at the amount of quixotic thoughts an eighteen year old girl could possibly process. It has three four whole years.

At lunch, I headed to the park bench and began to unravel the wrapping of my tuna sandwich when Margaret appeared. "Paige, you must go. Bret and I are going. You have to go with us. I know Travis hurt your feelings, but that shouldn't stop you from having the best night of your life!"

The best night of my life? I thought back to the day in grade six. The lights were off and the gymnasium sparkled. It was filled with innocent, joyful children who never knew heartbreak. These children felt nothing but bliss and butterflies. I was one of them. Blake walked right up to me and asked me to dance: my very first one. We were both real amateurs; he swayed left and I swayed right. We blurted out laughing in the middle of the chorus and blamed each other for that failure of a dance. Deep inside, we were glad it was with each other. I felt those lyrics synchronized to the pounding of my heart. Those five minutes felt like an eternity. The gymnasium was blasting loud music, popcorn flew everywhere and laughter filled the entire space. Yet all I could feel were butterflies. Many dances later, I still haven't felt that sort of bliss again.

"Are you even listening?" Margaret questioned my lack of interest.

"Yeah, sorry. I was just thinking."

"Of course! Probably about Blake," Margaret responded.

It always was. I had to get a grasp on reality. I knew Travis should be the one on my mind. Blake used to refer to me as "Pissy Paige" every time I angered him. Whenever he saw that even the slightest part of me was upset, he would squeeze me tight and whisper into my ears, "You know I love you, my perfect Paige."

It was grade eight and I did not trust my instincts nor did I trust his genuineness. Whatever we had, I believed it to be just some fling; a thing that every grade eight goes through. I was wrong. He apparently dated three girls after. Travis gave me clarity; he allowed me to see if I could try and move on. I couldn't. And that's when I knew it; I was still stuck in my past with Blake.

Just four days until prom night. I didn't have a dress and didn't plan on buying one. Margaret rang me every ten minutes begging me to go. Prom is about making special memories and creating those picturesque moments to hold onto forever. Prom is a night to feel special and to make others feel the same warmth, and light heartedness. It's a night to spend with the one you love, to dance, to laugh and cry of joy. It just won't be that way for me.

One night left. I tried to keep myself occupied by flipping through the innumerable biology notes for the test Monday. Yet, I could not fixate on any of the keywords that I had to know for the test Monday since my mind was all over the place.

Margaret called again with the same concerns: "You're saying there's no way you'll go? There's absolutely nothing I can do to get you to go?" Marg hung up instantly.

Of course there was a way. I tried my best not to fixate on my improbable fantasies. Yet prom was still hindering my thoughts about Monday's biology test. "Nope," I whispered to myself, loud enough for me to realize that I was struggling to convince myself to move on.

The morning of prom, I woke up to the sweet, soothing smell of the lavender bush. An old picture of me and Travis was lying beneath my chair. I picked it up and quickly noticed the absence of a real smile on my face. It wasn't always this way. I glanced repeatedly at the clock which seemed to also be telling me to "Go." It was nine o'clock, and I was late for first period.

At lunch, I took a long walk to the path in the forest beside our school; one where you could hear yourself breathe. I sat down at the dusty log table that was covered with graffiti swears. I underlined the huge pink heart on the table with my fingers, remembering that Travis and I were guilty of that inscription. We were supposedly madly in love. We inscribed the letters T+P on the bench in the middle of that dusty, pink heart. It means nothing now.

"Paige, why are you all alone here?" Travis spoke from behind. I jolted, not having heard his voice for quite a long time.

The last time we talked involved me apologizing for our failed relationship and simply walking away. Saying that sorry that day felt more relieving than upsetting as it wasn't fair for Travis to keep acting like there wasn't any problem.

"I wanted to talk to you about prom. I know you don't want to go, but I do. When we were together, I made these plans. I know we broke up because you realized the past was still too big of a part in your present. I could see you never felt the same way as I did. You never have. Your heart is still back in the old city, where Blake is. But as a friend, I'm requesting for you to join me to prom," Travis said with a smile.

He always knew me more than Marg did. He always tried. "Of course I will. You are, and will forever be, my best friend," I replied with a sense of reassurance and comfort.

In the limousine, on our way to prom, I finally managed to thank Travis for all he ever did for me.

"Thanks for what?" Travis questioned.

"Just everything," I replied.

Travis tried to make me laugh and dance the whole night. Every song brought me back to the promises Blake and I had made about this night. We had promised each other to share the excitement of this day four years ago. Blake promised that he would fly across the world to see me if for some reason I moved across the world for grade twelve. He said prom was ours. And here I was, alone. The words, "I love you," remained in the back of my head, hindering all other thoughts. I never said it. It was almost as if I ran away that night four years back, without saying goodbye or even acknowledging the fact I was leaving Blake behind forever.

I was quiet at dinner, yet my head was screaming with upsetting, impairing thoughts. I envied the fact that Marg and Bret got to share those three words with each other. I wiped away the one tear that made its way to the sleeve of my satin, blue gown, apologized to Travis for everything and ran across the banquet hall towards the main entrance. That was when the song "Fifteen" burst out of the speakers from all around the room.

    Everyone was on their feet now. I stood still in the center of the auditorium. The spotlight was shining on me, and Blake was standing across the way. I turned back towards my table and saw Travis beaming at me. At that moment I knew that Travis was the greatest friend a girl could ever ask for. Blake and I were now face to face. Blake placed his cold hand on my waist and took me in his arms: I swayed right, he swayed left. We chuckled at our lack of dancing skills. Even now, we were those two silly kids who could not help but smile at the sight of each other. Even now, we couldn't help but laugh. The past and the present became immaculately harmonized. At that exact moment, we were the same people we were four years ago. At that exact moment in time, we leaned forward, looked eye to eye, whispered the same exact words, and giggled.

RUNNER UP

Sunken

Celine N. Persaud

For a significant part of my childhood, I lived in Guyana – the only country in South America that is considered a member state of the Caribbean. In Guyana, children who attend school enjoy a two week Easter break. During Easter, it is traditional to fly kites on the sea wall. The sea wall is exactly what it sounds like – a concrete wall that separates the Atlantic Ocean from the coastland. Along this four feet tall wall that stretches for miles, kites of all colours, shapes, and sizes soar and sing in the wind-whipped sky. During sunset, they block the rays of the tangerine sun, which creates hundreds of dancing kite shadows. However, three years ago, we decided to spend our Easter elsewhere.

It is the morning of our trip, and I am the first person awake. As I lie in bed, I await a stir of movement from my parents and my brothers. The melodious chirps of the kisscadees, blue sackies, and robin red breasts are serene and rich like a harp's charm. I watch the sun as it dyes the clouds pink and I realize that it is now 6:30 a.m. and no one else has surfaced. I toss and turn and pack and pace and repack.

One excruciatingly long hour later we are all in the van – packed like a can of sardines and ready to go. Our adventure awaits! After cruising for approximately half of an hour, we arrive at the docks. I glance at the speedboat we are about to board and think to myself that this ride is going – to – be – interesting! As we speed along the bank of the Essequibo River,

I lightly bump up and down on my seat. Bravely, I walk up to the bow of the boat and stand there, embracing the fierce wind that beats against and caresses my face. My hair freely dances in the wind and in this moment, I feel as if I'm on top of the world. But what is that? Again I feel it. A raindrop. Two raindrops and three and four! As the rain begins to fall, the sky is encircled with grey clouds and the air becomes chilly. Within a few seconds, it is pouring.

My blissful moment of being on top of the world is given a taste of reality, and I'm now back on earth. Fear is instilled in everyone because we are on the river with no boats or docks in sight. Visibility slowly reduces. Luckily an abandoned dock, with a shelter similar to that of a hangar, is in sight. We huddle under there for what feels like ages.

As soon as the droplets turn to mist, we cross the river. Speeding along the bank of a river is simple, however, crossing a river can be fearsome because the boat is now sailing against the wave. It is nerve wracking and dangerous, especially when crossing at the mouth of the river which leads to the Atlantic Ocean. The boat swishes and dances from side to side in the choppy water, and suddenly I wish that boats were equipped with seatbelts.

By this time, the skies are once again clear, but turbulent waters still await. The boat and the water argue and fight and the water is winning. The waves slap the boat from side to side but the boat manages to brace itself after every blow. An uppercut blow hurls the bow of the boat about two feet into the air, and I grapple the seat in front of me for dear life.

"Dear God, please be here with us at this moment," I sincerely pray. "Please, please, please, please. I don't wanna die today. I can't even swim," I mumble.

Five minutes later, the boat and the water make amends. They now waltz like they are at a ballroom dance; in sync, they glide with each other. About three miles later, we arrive at our destination – the Hurukabra River Eco Resort.

As we tour the small resort, I am in awe of how exquisite simplicity can be. The thatch roof, made of dried but sturdy leaves, enhances the architecture of the resort's main building. The coconut trees create a warm and welcoming shade that could make anyone feel like they are on cloud nine. The longer I sit under them, the lazier I become.

In an effort to be productive and enjoy other activities, I join my family for a swim. Do note that we are not swimming in a pool – we are swimming in the river! The water is not like the rest of the Caribbean's average blue water. It is dark like a sopping wet velvet curtain, hiding all of the river's mystical creatures beneath it.

Aside from the fact that I am not a great swimmer, I decide to not swim because I – HATE – DARK – WATER. Instead, I opt out for sitting with my legs just dangling in the water. The cold water sends chilling ripples up my legs, and throughout my entire body. Today it is 23 degrees, scorching… the same as most days. Beads of sweat trickle down my temples and the arch of my back. Like a sponge, the water absorbs the heat that emanates off of my body. I daintily graze my toes back and forth against the water in an effort to savour this blissful feeling.

"Hey guys, take a look at this!" my elder brother, Charles says. He clambers onto a vine, swings like Tarzan and then plunges into the water.

"Woo, woo!" we all cheer and go back to our unwinding and our slumbering.

Ten seconds elapses and my mom begins to shriek. "He hasn't come up. He isn't coming up! MY SON! SOMEONE HELP HIM!"

Fear.

Fear is in everyone's facial expressions.

Suddenly, he surfaces, gasps for a most appreciated breath of air, and then plunders back into the water. This happens again and again and again. Three more times. My dad dives in to rescue him but he whacks his right leg against a little boat that is docked nearby and turns back.

"Is my brother going to drown at this moment? Please, somebody do something!" The words cannot escape the confines of my tightly shut lips. At this moment I am in shock. My fingers are now cold. My cheeks are cold. My lips are cold. I do not want to lose one of the dearest persons in my life – one that I hold closely to my heart. If his world stops, so will mine.

Out of nowhere, like the powerful hero Achilles, our boat's captain dives into the water to rescue my brother! He disappears under the water and several seconds later he emerges. There! I see my brother's head. His neck. Now his arms. As they swim back to shore, my heart beat begins to slow down, blood rushes back to my face, I no longer hold my breath, I breathe a sigh of relief.

He is breathless. He is scared. He is tired. But he is still alive.

I hug him tightly, not wanting to let go – my entire perspective of life and its value changes at this very moment. As the daunting thought that I could have just lost my brother lingers, I promise myself that I will, never again, swim in dark water or even set foot near it. It is as if the dark water, or as we call it, "Black Water", is really what it sounds like. Whenever I look at it, it screams "evil" to me. I cannot comprehend why he almost drowned; he is a really good swimmer.

As he describes his experience to me, he says, "It was as if something was holding me down and didn't want to let go."

As queer as that sounds, it surely sets off a thousand fireworks in my brain.

GRADES 9 - 10

1st PLACE

Warzone

Ellen Zhang

I love you.
I hate you.
Can you tell the difference?
Love and hate are often described as opposites, yet why do they sound so alike? It might as well be the same thing. After all, they're both uncontrollable, intriguing, and fully capable of taking over a major part, if not all of our lives. They bring us joy, satisfaction, false happiness, and let's not forget pain… the soul tearing pain. In other words, it can be the fuel that keeps us alive or the devouring power that consumes us.

They're so alike, but they are not meant to co-exist.
Why?
Because it's life, that's why.
But is it possible to love someone as much as you hate him?

In our minds, there's a fine line between love and hate; a border that's supposed to keep the calm in the chaos. A wall that exists as an attempt to maintain the peace within us.

However, life is unpredictable, and peace is fragile. The moment it is disturbed… is the moment you turn into a warzone.

We become the object of corruption. Love and hate forms a battlefield, they fight and make sacrifices. They do everything… anything to conquer you.

Warzone

If we go back to the question; is it possible to love someone as much as you hate him? The answer is, yes. It is absolutely possible.

...But will you be able to live through the war?

* * * * *

I, Wendy, currently have three wishes. It might seem like a lot, but wishes are like dreams... they're free, sometimes out of our reach, yet they give us just enough hope to keep us moving. It's the kind of luxury everyone can afford. That's why I can shamelessly allow myself to wish...

One...
I wish I never met him.

Dante created too many 'ifs' in my life. If, on that day I hadn't overslept, I wouldn't have had to rush to school. Then I wouldn't have crashed into him and uttered my apologies. If that never happened, then maybe I wouldn't have heard that enchanting voice that assured me everything was fine. There would have been no fateful first meeting. And if we hadn't met, then maybe he wouldn't have taken a seat next to me. If that never happened, then maybe he wouldn't have noticed me. If I, by nature, was less curious, then I wouldn't have turned to look at him. I would've been able to resist the temptation to let my gaze wander over the new face. If my eyes had been elsewhere that moment, that one moment, then I wouldn't have caught the sight of him smiling... and become totally captivated.

Two...
I wish I was stronger.

If I was stronger then I wouldn't have fallen so hard so easily. He wouldn't have been able to pull me in so deep. If I was *stronger, I would've been able to break free from his invisible chains and free myself from his grasp. If I was stronger, I wouldn't have made the mistake of offering him my heart on a silver platter.*

Three...
I wish to live.

Dante... shall we live through war?

* * * * *

Wendy looked down at the pot of stew. The aroma from the steam has vanished and left a cold and untouched dish along with another broken promise.

Wendy had been prepared for it. One would think that by now, she would be used to the disappointment that flooded over her. The feeling of dejection filled her lungs, suffocating her. But somewhere deep down inside, there was a corner illuminated by a ray of hope; one that had yet to be blown out by the darkness.

Dante had given her his promise, and that's why she allowed herself to smile, let that dangerous feeling of warmth spread behind her ribcage. It was always like this. One moment she would be soaring, but once the realization set in, she always found herself fighting to stay afloat.

Perhaps she shouldn't feel this dejected. After all, it was only a dinner. Another meal out of so many.

* * * * *

Despite living in the same house and enrolling in the same university, the two of them barely saw each other. Wendy was a Physics major, while Dante majored in Music.

Science and art were in different buildings on two different ends of campus, as if to make sure that the clashing subjects would never meet. Not even by coincidence. Perhaps it was believed that balance and peace could only be achieved by separation. That coexistence was only possible if there was a wall between them. Like two chambers of the heart, belonging to one, but forbidden to interact.

Still, Wendy couldn't help but sometimes wander across the lawn, just to catch a quick glimpse of the person who was so close, yet so far from her.

It had been apparent from the very start that the sound of Dante's heart beats would never match her own. Yet Wendy couldn't deter her human instincts, and from time to time she allowed herself to believe that she was, in a way, special. Irreplaceable.

She allowed herself to be foolish.

* * * * *

The long hours of silence should have been the cue for Wendy to get up, but something kept her in place, her eyes stubbornly glued to the front door that wouldn't open. The hurried steps on the stairs let her eagerly anticipate the metallic sound of a key turning. But it never came.

She wondered if it was always going to be like this. Just when she thought she was ready to give up, something would once again nurture that seed of hope she thought she'd lost.

Whenever she thought: 'Ah, I should get out of here,' perhaps find her own place, something made her stay: a genuine smile, a pat on the shoulder, a glimpse of Dante's caring nature asking her to stay.

It had been a long time since Wendy had realized that she would do anything Dante asked her to…

* * * * *

Wendy turned her head to look at the clock again and finally the sound of keys jingling filled the silent room. Unconsciously, her body froze waiting for the moment Dante's face would appear through the front door. But again she was unable to foresee, no matter how many times she faced it, the high-pitched giggle along with the low chuckle that undoubtedly belonged to Dante.

Dante and his female companion staggered through the door. It slammed shut after them.

Another kiss, another laugh, and Wendy's breath hitched. What was it that made her suffocate like this? To dodge and to run, what was it that prevented her from doing so?

Her eyes stung at the sight of the enemy.

Wendy felt her hands clench on her sides, her bitten nails dug into flesh. It hurt, but it was nothing compared to the emotion that rushed through her at the sight of them.

It wasn't until they thought to move towards the bedroom, they noticed her. A little lost and wounded, she stood alone in the midst of it all.

"You're still up?" Dante wasn't surprised, even though he tried to sound like it.

She had to turn her head away momentarily because neither Dante nor the girl had the decency to adjust their inappropriate attire. "You waited up for me." Wendy couldn't help but to turn back at that. In her eyes there was only Dante, a beautiful creature who hadn't even bothered to mask his attack in the form of a question.

Wendy's gaze shifted over to the girl who was tugging impatiently at Dante's unbuttoned shirt. Long brown hair, clear porcelain skin and a petite frame, she matched perfectly with the girls she had seen with Dante on previous nights.

Wendy shook her head.

"I wasn't," was all she could say. It was weak and pathetic, but she wasn't sure she could live with herself if she didn't even put a small ounce of effort in defending what pride she had left. "Why would I?" She made an attempt to sneer.

The nameless girl seemed to finally acknowledge her presence as she asked, "Who's this?"

"Oh, this?" Dante's eyes crinkled. "My close friend and roommate, Wendy."

It wasn't until Dante said it out loud that Wendy realized they had never been close. Not really. Dante wouldn't let anyone close to him.

Dante bent slightly to place a kiss on the young woman's cheek, and Wendy's heart skipped a beat for all the wrong reasons. The giggling scraped her skin with its sharp edges.

"Let's go to your room. She might kick you out if we stay here." The girl grabbed Dante's hand and started to pull at it.

But Dante's eyes were fixed on his friend, knowing and empowered. "She won't." His clear voice marked the ending of something unknown… the time of waiting was over and slowly they were entering a new phase.

"She's in love with me." The smirk adorning Dante's features made Wendy's inside twist and turn. With barely any effort, Wendy was left permanently marred.

She crept into bed and buried herself under the blanket with a silent prayer to rapidly fall asleep.

She had started innocent, young, and naïve as she stepped into a conflict she knew absolutely nothing about.

Dante…

I hate you…

…I love you.

2nd PLACE

From Frost Comes Flowers

Crystal Lu

We all started out small, plain and simple, like seeds. Even crying and pink-faced, we were miracles. From those seeds, we were to grow into the tall, strong people were were meant to be. The people we were supposed to be. We would stretch our hands up and touch the sky. Nothing would hold us back.

Finally, we sprouted. Our roots sunk into the earth, as our delicate branches reached out.

I took a long time to grow, just like an oak tree. You waited for me anyway.

We were frail.

We laughed and ran like there was no tomorrow.

We were innocent.

We pretended to be knights fighting dragons, bound ourselves together with bracelets and pinky promises.

We were happy.

Nothing mattered.

We did everything we wanted with no regrets, dreaming about the future, a concept we barely grasped at the time. We dozed off after long days, in the warm glow of a butterfly nightlight, still wrapped in the arms of your mum. Our protector.

Years passed, and our branches began to stretch out further. We were stronger, but not by much.

We were still together, arm in arm. We met new friends, but no one could truly separate us. We were two peas in a pod. We learned what we were good at and what we were less than great at.

Nothing mattered. That night at your house, we danced in our PJs like no one was watching. We promised each other that we would never let go. No one could hurt us. We would be each other's maids of honour when we were older. The promise of sisterhood.

We were happy.

Our branches strengthened and bark started forming as we became teenagers. That's when we put on masks, pretending to be people we weren't. We said things that we regretted. We did things that we could never forget. We convinced ourselves that we were okay when we weren't. We didn't know who we were and where we were going.

Nothing mattered. We were in this together.

That was the year that I had to survive winter on my own.

Your chilly words wore down on my bark, destroying my protection. Frost enveloped me, as I was left frozen and alone. People laughed at me for being different. People laughed at me because I was myself. They haunted me worse than the monsters that were under my bed as a kid. Sticks and stones were nothing compared to the words. They were awful. The sticks left temporary cuts.

The words settled and scarred.

But nothing was worse than my very own demons, lurking in the shadows of my mind. No one could stop them. They were always there. I didn't want to give in, but they wouldn't leave me alone.

I fell in love that year. It was a temporary bliss. I loved him, and I was convinced that he loved me back.

I was happy. Or so I thought.

I was the last one to know that he had been seeing someone else. I caught them in the courtyard, kissing under the trees. My heart felt like he had ripped it out and stomped on it, before he threw it away. I choked back the tears and ran. I cried in my room alone when I got home.

I was a wreck.

That year, my mum and dad started yelling at me, and at each other. It felt like a warzone, where words crashed and burned. I didn't realize that they were slowly being sawed away from each other.

They decided split up.

I was withering away. I wanted to run away and hide. But I couldn't.

I felt trapped.

Nothing mattered because I couldn't do anything.

I was sad.

I thought I would never heal. But I did in the end.

I thought I was frozen, almost dead on the inside, but after a couple of years, something started to flicker inside me. The air became warmer. Everything became lighter. I was taller and sturdier.

I thawed.

My mind no longer held me back. I had the freedom I desired, and I was at peace with myself. I no longer had the weak skimpy branches I had before. I had a thick trunk and husky branches, wrapped in tough bark. My bark had scars from growing up, but because of them, I was stronger.

I wouldn't be myself without them.

I was the oak tree that survived a storm.

I was happy.

I finally saw you again. You were broken. Those girls who promised you happiness tore you down into little bits, and left you all alone in the dark. You were crying. Your bark had been ripped off, clean. You only had a few branches left, and most of them were damaged. You told me that you were wrong to trust them, and that you were sorry. You told me that it was all your fault, and that you would understand if I never wanted to see you again.

I could've left you.

But I didn't.

I saw your fear. I saw that what you thought you wanted wasn't really what you imagined it to be. I saw your hopes and dreams of being happy crumbling, like rocks washing away into the ocean. You looked at me, as if you were dangling off a cliff, and I was the only one who could save you.

You had no one, and I knew that you would break completely if no one helped you. You left me, but you didn't deserve this. No one deserves to be left in the dark, no matter how deeply they fell into the shadows.

It was always us.

I held your hand and pulled you back up.

It took time, but it was worth it. Your bark became resilient, and your branches slowly mended themselves.

You, the white pine, could finally reseed after being burnt down.

You grew until you were as tall as me. Our branches intertwined, just like how our arms were always woven together.

Our branches were sturdy from the scars that hid beneath the skin. They were no longer frail.

We laughed and ran like we were still innocent.

Even if we fell apart all those years ago, we were still bound together.

And we grew, and grew.

Until it was your wedding day.

You stood by the altar, and I wasn't next to you as your maid of honour.

You smiled at me. I smiled back.

You were radiant.

You were decked in pure white. Fiery marigolds were laced into your hair, and a glowing smile graced your lips.

Distant echoes of music sounded in my head as I floated down the aisle. The notes swirled into the air and became a blur as I approached you. I paused at the altar, and for the first time, you held my hands. Vows were exchanged, eternally binding us to a life of love and companionship. We would never be alone. When we embraced, we became one. We were no longer bound by bracelets or pinky promises. We were united by rings of glittering diamonds that would last forever.

That was the start of our new beginning.

We could finally touch the sky.

And we were happy.

3rd PLACE

Through War We Endure

Lily de Loë

The walls will shake.
The bombs will fall.
And the pianist –
the pianist will play on.

* * * * *

    There once was a city shrouded in smoke, and the people tried their best to quell the flames. Dust was their uniform, sirens their anthem. And rubble? Rubble was their home – or at least what was left of one.

    London, its streets shrouded in silence each night. A once lively city, now devoid of lights shining in its windows and headlight beams tracing paths down its streets. Illumination is provided solely by fire. Flames illuminated craters and occasionally the blackened carcass of a double decker bus. How eerie and empty, those streets. Stripped of the civilians who lay sleeping, hidden away in the depths below.

    Some were willing to believe that the air raid shelters could weather the wrath of the Nazi regime. Others, meanwhile, were wary and sceptical. They knew – knew – that while darkness hid the living from the bombers, their pilots would still be aware that a city sat just below their cockpits.

    Those German bombers, the damage they did was unfathomable. Whole neighbourhoods were reduced to rubble in the course of mere hours. Or what felt like hours. Time seems to still when the walls shake so violently that you feel they're coming down around you.

* * * * *

Hidden below the streets was a girl in a pale blue dress, her light brown hair secured in a bow. She sat in an air raid shelter, watching the overhead bulb swing back and forth on its wire, like a pendulum. How real the war now seemed to her, how unbelievably different from anything she ever could have imagined.

So unalike those toy soldiers and war games that the boys had played before. In games, there was never actual destruction, and it was never uncertain that the good soldiers would win. The impact of a bomb shook the shelter, causing her to stifle a sob. Those glorified games would never have taken her father from her.

The impact stirred many from their sleep. Bulbs flickered, and if the ceiling had been plaster, chunks of it would have fallen in a cloud of dust. The blast had been close, the closest one yet. She could feel her heart beating hard, as if it were attempting to escape from her chest.

The girl's mother sat next to her, coaxing her back to sleep. Soft words of reassurance spoken in the dark of the night. A scratchy wool blanket wrapped around her shoulders. The squeezing of her hand, slackening as exhaustion dragged the woman back into sleep.

The girl remained sitting, awake while others slept. Arms hugging her legs, eyes on that flickering, swaying bulb. Surrounded by silence, if not for the sound of her breath and the slow drip of water. Sleep did not come easily that night.

When sleep eventually came, her dreams were plagued by Nazis. They flew over the city, laughing as they turned her house to dust. They came in ships, on foot, in terrible machines. They tinted the sea crimson and stalked her as if they were cats and she a mouse. Their destruction turned the sky black and snuffed out the stars. She plummeted into the abyss, and in its depths pulsed a steady chant of "Heil Hitler". But then, she stopped.

The sound of a piano, it broke the chant and allowed the stars to shine once more. The melody was disembodied, as if broadcast to the entire world. Even in her dreams she would recognize its source: the pianist.

* * * * *

The blitz would last fifty-seven days. Throughout it, the people of London would see eleven pianos, but only one set of hands. Something so simple, but still, a shred of normality amidst the chaos of an ever-changing London. The physical appearance of those hands would change – cloaked in fingerless gloves on a particularly cold day or nails bitten to the quick after a particularly stressful night – and yet, they would never cease to perform the same graceful motions atop the keys. The pianist was the epitome of endurance during wartime.

Endurance would be everywhere. It was in the smallest of actions, most commonly in the ability to get up each morning. With jobs and families, some had no other choice but to leave the shelters and find some way to carry on. He, however, had no employer.

The poor man looked forever tired, albeit punctual despite his tired manner. But fatigue aside, as long as the streets filled, he would play for the masses. To passersby, something about his demeanour seemed to age him beyond his years. Not decrepit exactly, but past his prime and certainly well past the age for enlistment. If his white hair did not reveal his age, perhaps his posture would. Hunched, the passage of time sat upon his shoulders and leached the colour from his hair. Wrinkles traced the planes of his face and the palms of his hands.

Whether he was too old to work or too rich to need to, no one knew. However, he provided hope to the home front, and for that people were grateful.

And what of the music itself? The pieces were always classical, elegant works that had long since been committed to memory. His mind held an extensive repertoire, luckily, as sheet music was rendered useless by the wind. He played with his eyes closed, and flecks of ash accumulated on his eyelashes.

It was truly a pity that the girl heard his music so few times.

* * * * *

During the first days of the blitz, he had played in Battersea and on his own instrument. The upright had been made of a dark, rich wood. The keys had scuffed edges, the pedals tilted from use. It had been slightly out of tune, but better than many he'd come to play. After all, piano tuners are scarce during wartime.

In the beginning, people had been confused by the piano sitting out by the street. It was as if the instrument had come out of nowhere. Still, it took less than a day to accept that regardless of how the piano had come to its current location, the music he played kept morale high. They clung to that music like a lifeline.

Word spread, and when one instrument was destroyed, a new one would appear in another area of the city. Most were donated by widows and grieving mothers. For these women some possessions simply held too many memories. Especially pianos, it seemed.

This was how many of the instruments came to sit on sidewalks, street corners, or wherever else there was room. The donors knew that even if their piano survived the bombings, they'd forever avert their eyes in its presence. At least with someone else at its keys, the fleeting memories and phantom melodies would cease, replaced with real, audible hope.

The girl, fast asleep in her air raid shelter, would emerge the next morning to find neither the pianist nor his music. That first piano had survived only three days before being reduced to a heap of charred wood and twisted strings.

In those first days, the residents of Battersea saw buildings flattened into the earth, the piano crushed beneath the debris. She'd search for it, of course, but without success. The old man now played in another neighbourhood, taking his music with him.

And in that new area of London, Chopin was reverberating off buildings and crumbling facades – Scherzo No.1, just audible above the din. A new audience would soon be enthralled by his steady crescendo, his light melodies.

To live, to keep face and do their duty to aid the war effort: that was the purpose of the home front. But of course, it is hard to keep face when one is powerless to prevent the bombs from falling.

Many would become casualties of war. If not by bombs, perhaps by their aftermath – collapsed ceilings, burst water mains and panic that led to deadly chaos. People were simply collateral damage standing in the path to victory. However, some did not await death, instead choosing to fight. Not by taking up arms, but by combating the despair that plagued the despondent and the grieving.

The pianist would play out the entirety of the blitz. No bomb could silence the music he played. As long as there was a need for hope, the pianist would play on.

RUNNER UP

Colour Blind

Khloe Henderson

Gray.

That was Margot's world. Everything was gray. Colour did not exist to her. Not yet.

Ever since she was young, her mother had told her about The Colours. Margot's mother saw them the first time she and Margot's father touched; that was what happened when you met your soulmate. A gray life would flourish at the first touch. Margot's mother said the colours were beautiful. They were like icing on a cake, or butter on popcorn, or freshly washed sheets. They made everything better. Margot's mother loved The Colours; she said they made waking up in the morning worthwhile. Margot's mother wasn't the only one – others saw them, too, and by the way everyone talked about "The Colouring" it sounded like a fairy tale come true.

Margot knew all the names of the basic colours by the time she was six, though she had no idea what they looked like. When she was eight, her mother told her about more colours like, teal, magenta and lilac; she forgot most of the others' names.

Along with the joy of colour there was sadness, too. Stories were told about old women who had lost their soulmates and lived in faded colour. Some, about men who never found love because they blocked the colour from their lives and were condemned to a forever gray world.

When Margot was young her mother often told her the story of the Gray Maiden – once there was a young woman who yearned for someone to love, for someone to colour her world. She spent every day dreaming of colour and how magical it must be. One day she was walking down a busy street; as she strode past a brisk-walking businessman, their hands brushed and the young woman's world burst to life in miraculous colour. She immediately spun on her heels and ran back to find the man. When she caught up to him she took his hand in hers, "Do you see it? It's so beautiful!" she said with a smile, looking around and then back at him.

"What are you talking about?" he said, pulling his hand away.

Nothing changed for him. And so, the colours could not remain for her.

The woman was forced to live her life, forever, gray.

"What if I never find him? What if I turn out like the Gray Maiden?" she asked her mother one night after the story. She had just turned twelve.

"You will, dear. I promise," she said, tucking a lock of curly hair behind Margot's ear.

* * * * *

Margot was seventeen and two of her friends, Isabel and Ada, were leaving in search of their soulmates. It was the summer they all graduated. That was what so many people did. They felt a calling to a certain place and when they returned they had their soulmate. Margot had never felt a calling to anywhere, but if she did, she hoped it would be to somewhere beautiful.

It was fairly cool in Roseville the day they both left. The summers were never hotter than 21 degrees. They were going to meet up at Terra Café; her favourite place, ever. Margot arrived first and stepped out of the wind, tossing a curly tress of hair over her shoulder. She ordered Earl Gray tea and smiled at the barista as she took her drink off the counter. Margo sat in the high chairs by the window and waited for her friends.

The glass had fogged up from the cool air outside as it mingled with the warm air of the Café. She blew steam off her drink and it fogged up her glasses. Margot nuzzled her nose into her scarf and let herself drift. She snapped out of it when the bell that hung over the door jingled.

Ada and Isabel waved to her and made a bee-line for the counter to order their own hot drinks, and then joined Margot. They enjoyed the privacy of being the only ones in the shop, other than the cashier, the barista and some guy mopping the floor; they all smiled at each other.

"So are you exited?" Margot asked them.

"Yes!" Ada said, putting her drink down, "I'm so excited, I actually think I might be sick!"

"I know!" Isabel said. "With all the butterflies in my stomach, I may take flight!"

They all laughed. Ada told the girls that her calling was to Greece. Isabel shared that she was off to Australia; she was drawn to it and all its marsupial glory. Margot said how much she was going to miss them; making them all cry a little bit. The rest of the afternoon was absorbed through re-lived childhood stories and reckless laughter. The friends all hugged goodbye and promised to call as often as possible; then they were gone. Margot went home and cried while her mom held her until she fell into a restless sleep.

Over the summer, Margot began working at her mother's flower shop. She regretted it because it seemed the only people who ever came in were happy soulmates. It made her feel foolish when she let it get to her. Whenever it became too much she would escape across the street to Terra. She would sit in the window and drink tea, sometimes reading, until she calmed down. One day a voice broke into her thoughts.

"Hey."

Margot turned to see the guy who mopped the floor leaning over the counter, looking at her. "Hi," she said back in a dismissive tone.

"I can't help but notice how often you come in here and how much tea you drink."

"Oh, I just come here whenever work gets to be too much for me," she said, turning back to her book.

"Where do you work?" he asked.

"Shut up," Margot thought, but she answered anyway, not wanting to be rude. "At Demeter's Flower Shoppe, across the street." She pointed out the window.

"Intense," he said with a laugh.

Margot reluctantly laughed too.

* * * * *

There was a blizzard the night the call came from Ada. It had been six months since they left, and it was about the hundredth phone call they had all shared. After Margot picked up, Ada added Isabel to the conversation. Together they cried when Ada told her story about meeting Charlie. They melted when Isabel told them about Graham. They announced they were coming home in a few weeks, soulmates in tow.

Margot was overjoyed and then, again, worried about finding her own soulmate. She knew that she needed the colours to truly live, because the gray was forcing her merely to exist. Margot didn't just see gray, she felt gray. She worried that she was waiting around for something that would never come. Margot knew it was possible never to find your soulmate and to stay gray forever. The thought brought fear into her chest.

That night she asked her mother, "What if I never find the one?"

Her mother hugged her and told her not to worry, that when she did find her soulmate all the waiting would be worth it.

Margo pushed the fear down and decided to stop feeling sorry for herself.

* * * * *

Eventually, the annoyance of the flower shop dissipated, and Margot began to truly love her job. She felt contentment amidst all the happy soulmates, the smell of the flowers early in the morning, the smiles of the people she served and the tea breaks she took every afternoon. She was even able to tolerate the constant interruptions of her solitude by the mop guy, Xavier.

Finally, the day came when Ada and Isabel returned home! The girls decided to meet up at Terra. Margot was excited to see her friends and hear about their countless adventures in soulmate searching. She woke up late and threw her jeans on, pulled a thick sweater over her head and strung her scarf around her neck. Snow blew in the door as Margot entered the café, still managing to arrive before Ada and Isabel.

Margot noticed Xavier was not mopping the floor but, instead, standing behind the till. She walked over and greeted him.

"Hey, you have a new job today?" Margot enquired.

"Yeah, Marie got a calling, and the barista doesn't start until two," Xavier replied. "So, it's just me, for now. Makes me grateful it's not so busy in here all the time. Anyways, what can I get you?"

"London Fog," she said, "extra hot."

"That'll be $2.49, please," he replied with a smile.

Colour Blind

Margot pushed a five dollar bill across the counter. The bell over the door jingleed, and Ada and Isabel's laughter fill the café. She smiled and held out her hand for the change. Xavier placed the coins in her hand, gently touching her palm. She felt something electric.

Margot looked at Xavier, and she knew she was looking into the bluest eyes she would ever see.

RUNNER UP

Deception

Sarah Demary

Josie never understood how people could expect the unexpected. She certainly couldn't. Why couldn't I have seen right through his pretty face? she asked herself every day, remembering who had put her there, who had ruined her life, her future. She had lost everything. She could never run again, she would never be looked at the same, she could never show her face at school, and most of all she had lost someone she truly loved.

The vibrating of her phone interrupted her thoughts. She turned her head slightly to the side and gazed up the phone to see who it was calling her. She bit down on her lip and cringed. Even to turn on her side it hurt too much. "Ow," she mumbled before finally being able to pick up her phone. When she saw who it was, her face drained of all its blood; her face sagged and she had begun to feel utterly distraught. "Josh." She gritted his name through her teeth and pressed the red end button then tossed her phone further down her bed. "Ow!" She yelled this time.

"Josie?" Her mother threw open the door with worried eyes.

"I'm okay mom, just threw my phone and forgot about my bruised arm." Josie tried smiling to cover her pain, to show her mom that she was okay even though she wasn't, but it was no use, the cringe she was trying so hard to hide showed through her fake smile. Her face was covered in the dried up tears that she had shed not too long ago when she was alone; Josie was clearly hurt, yet she did not want to show it.

"Josie, you just got out of the hospital. I don't want you ending up back there again because you couldn't follow simple orders," her mom said, her arms folded against her chest. "The doctor said to take it easy, and don't worry, the police will find out who did this."

Josie frowned. "I already know who did this; Nick did this."

Her mother sighed and rolled her eyes for what seemed like the billionth time since the incident. "Josie, I told you, Nick could not have done this. He's been out of town all week."

Josie rolled her eyes this time out of disbelief.

"Why would Nick do something as horrible like that anyways? He loved you."

Of course she chose his side; the so called "saint" always got the approval of mother, Josie thought. Her mother always approved of everyone she dated but when it came to Nick, she thought he would be the 'one' for her.

"You know why, mom." Josie didn't want to bring this up, but she wanted her mom to see the truth.

"You can't blame him for leaving, Josie. He's seventeen, and he isn't ready for that kind of commitment. But he would never do something like that to you."

Josie laid back on her pillow and ignored her mom, not wanting to get into another argument. "Could you get my phone out of here please? Josh has called seven times in the past ten minutes, and I'm tired of having to press the end button every five seconds." It even hurt for her to speak.

"Okay, but you have a visitor." Her mother grabbed Josie's phone from her bed and walked away with it, letting the visitor right in.

There he stood at a decent 5'9", black thin hair that curved over to the side at the front, giving him that Boo Boo Stewart look, is what Josie told him when they first met. He was partially tanned and had emerald eyes. His tight shirt outlined his muscular figure and brought out his ginormous arms. He attempted a slight smile before having it turned down by Josie's death glare.

"Did hanging up on you not tell you that we are done?" Josie hissed.

"And did my obsessive calls not tell you that I am not giving up," Josh said with a smirk on his face, a smirk that still made Josie melt inside whenever she saw it.

She whipped her head to the side to keep herself from staring, regretting it seconds later. "Ow," she said softly.

Josh raced over to her and tried touching her, but Josie found enough strength to swat his hand away.

"Josie, how many times do I have to tell you that it wasn't my fault?"

Josie sighed, annoyed, and pulled herself up slowly into a sitting position. "How could you? I said that if you told him anything I was as good as dead!" Josie reached over for her water and took a sip.

Josh held a confused face; he had no idea what Josie was going on about. "What?" he finally asked.

"I was put in the hospital because your buddy knew. You told him, and he rammed my car into a tree with his damn truck. Now you tell me, why in the hell would he do that if he didn't know? He could have killed me, Josh, and as far as I know he still thinks he did." Josie's pale face was now burning red out of anger and her throat hurt even more from all that yelling. "Nick did this? I'm going to kill that bastard."

Josh gritted his teeth. "For what? For not getting the job done?"

A tear fell down Josie's face. Josh sat on the bed, centimetres away staring right into her blue eyes. He smiled and moved a strand of her red hair from her face. "You really don't remember, do you?" Josh lowered his head and shook it. This time Josie was the one to look confused. "Now, Josie, how could I have been in on this if I was in the car with you as well."

Josh revealed his bruised chest and legs as proof, and Josie gasped, not believing that her boyfriend was in the car with her at the time of the incident.

"I blacked out before I could get a look at our attempted murder. I was up to see the car flip midair and I was out as soon as the car dropped." Josie pushed herself up and against her bed, shaking her head out of disbelief. Who would want to kill us then, she asked herself. It was obviously not an accident. There were only two people that were ashamed of what Nick and her had done six months ago… and that's when it came to her. Unlike Josh, she got to see who flipped their car. He walked over to the car to see if he got the job done He checked and saw their closed eyes, and then Josie opened hers and watched as he ran away.

She had misunderstood the whole situation and him. She had it all wrong. Nick didn't run them over, she had it all confused. Nick and her broke up five months ago. She told him that she was falling in love with him, and he couldn't handle that. A month later Josh and her became an item, and that's when her big secret came out. A secret that she and three others knew. Everything was starting to come to her again. Nick didn't do it. He couldn't have.

"Daddy…" Josie whispered under her breath. Tears slowly glided down her cheek and her heart rate began to decrease. He didn't go on a business trip, he ran away from what he did. She remembered seeing his black work boots approach her broken body and crunch against the shattered glass of all the cars mirrors, the car that he had helped her pick out, the car that he spent half his savings on. She remembered watching him drive off in his blue Chevy Colorado, while she called for him in pain. He was the one person who didn't show up to the hospital that day, the one person who walked out the door as soon as she revealed that she was pregnant with Nick's child.

"Who?" Josh leaned in closer to her so he could hear her better.

"My Dad killed my baby."

RUNNER UP

Pursuit of Love

Sabrina La

Have you ever wanted someone badyly, so badly that your hands shook, your eyes twitched and your heart became erratic in their presence? That someone was like a shining beacon, luring you in and never letting go?

For me, that someone was Alexander DeCaro, my wildest and most impossible fantasy. He rarely spoke to anyone and held himself in a secluded way. No one could figure him out, nor did they want to.

I was the only exception.

I remember that it happened at the beginning of senior year. I was turning the corner to get to my English class when we barrelled into each other and he caught me before I could tumble to the floor. Totally cliché, right? Except, instead of love at first sight or before I could even thank him, he had sighed and disappeared out of my sight – he was always one with the shadows.

Since then, I'd never had the nerve to approach him, but the flicker of curiosity in me scorched into a flame as time went on, threatening to burn me up. A part of me warned that there was a reason he was so secluded, but another part of me – the more dominating force – focused only on his deep eyes and angelic face.

Who cared if he was more like a demon?

* * * * *

"Anna. Hey Anna. Connie!" I cringed as the final word out of my friend's mouth reached my ears.

"It's Constance, Anna or Constance. Never... Connie." I mock shuddered, while eyeing my friend and lab partner warily.

Zanella flicked her dyed hair over her shoulder and continued measuring the solutions in the test tubes, pretending she didn't hear me.

"So... you thinking about Alexander again?" she asked casually. I cringed under her scrutiny as I felt her eyes on me. It had been four months since our first and last encounter, and she knew I was still obsessing over it – him, but I refused to admit it. If I revealed my thoughts and feelings about him to Zanella, it seemed as if I was letting my closely guarded secret free – something that I was not ready to do yet.

From the sigh Zanella let out, she knew it too.

"Whatever," she finally said. "Let's just finish mixing these chemicals and cross our fingers for an explosion."

* * * * *

It was a typical start to a Wednesday morning... up until I got kidnapped.

I pulled into the student parking lot and not a minute after I stepped out of my car, a blindfold went over my eyes and I was being dragged backwards. I heard heavy breathing, felt soft hands on my arms, and most importantly smelled the familiar fragrance of hair-dye.

"Zanella? What are you doing?" I struggled in her grasp, though I trusted her and didn't think she'd hurt me.

"Shh, almost there," she whispered. I relaxed at the sound of her soothing voice and eventually relented to having her pull me wherever she was going.

A short moment later, I heard a door creak open. I was led inside, and then it slammed shut.

"Okay, take your blindfold off!" she called from the other side of the door, her voice muted.

I did, and the sight in front of me had me reeling back and hitting the door. There, a mere five feet away, stood Alexander. Like me, he was also gripping a blindfold in hand, his face looking as shocked as I felt.

"Now," Zanella started, "Alexander, tell her what you need to. I'm not unlocking this door until you do." Her voice held a hint of triumph, but I was already planning the ways I'd make her regret it afterwards. In vain, I tried the handle, but she was right: it was locked from the outside.

"Well," I said, spinning to face Alexander, "tell me what you need to so we can get out of here." I didn't know where the sudden burst of confidence came from, nor did I mean to be so rude to the boy I was crushing on, but between being betrayed by my friend and being trapped in a room with said boy, I was on the verge of a panic attack.

Alexander stared at me warily for a second, and I didn't know how I managed to do it, but I stared right back. He looked good: worn sweater, jeans, and his signature sneakers. It was the first time that I had a chance to stare openly at him, and trapped or not, I was not wasting this opportunity.

"Um…" his first word pulled me from my reverie. I snapped my eyes back to his face and just caught a hint of blush on his sharp cheekbones before he became Mr. Cold-And- Mysterious again. "I'm sorry we had to meet this way. And I didn't plan on telling you like this, but if I don't do it now… Well, Anna, I really like you. Would you like to go on a date with me?"

For the first few seconds, I stared at him blankly. Then all at once, heat rushed into my face and a dull buzz hummed in my head. I raised my hand and knocked on the door.

"Zanella, he told me what he needed to. Open up."

In a trance, I heard the door unlock, and without a word to either of them, I pulled it open and walked away.

* * * * *

"Anna. Hey, Anna. Connie!" I snapped my attention back to the table in front of me and glared at my best friend.

"It's Constance," I repeated for what seemed like the millionth time in our friendship.

"Actually," a voice murmurs beside me, "It's DeCaro now."

I smile at my husband. "Right. Sorry. It's automatic now."

Alex just chuckles and pulls me into his side.

"So what were you thinking about there?" asked Zanella. She hasn't changed one bit since high school.

"Just how Alex and I met," I revealed, giving her a pointed look.

"C'mon, Anna. It's been five years. Plus, it worked out anyways, didn't it?"

She was right. After I left to clear my head, I realized that despite the overwhelmed state I was in, Alex didn't deserve to be treated that way. He was the one who had the courage to admit his feelings, and under all my disbelief and shock, I was… euphoric.

My angel had revealed himself at last.

After school, I found him to apologize and asked if he was still up for that date. We ended up at a corner café where we talked the night away. I learned that he had been heartbroken before and was reluctant to become vulnerable with someone else again. I vowed then to never make him regret his decision.

Five years of being a happy couple later, we got married.

Pursuit of Love

'Yes," I squeeze Alex's hand in mine, replaying our first conversation again in my mind. It wasn't the most common way to find your soul mate, but it worked for us. "It did."

RUNNER UP

Dawn

Holly Lavergne

You stand on the back porch, staring. You stare almost blankly, into the mist. The lingering raindrops that take their time, forming spheres, ovals, teardrops, and falling into oblivion; they surround you. The wooden slats are cold beneath your bare feet. You lean peacefully against the railing, dew glistening on its surface. It is just past six in the morning.

You are four years old. You climbed out of the restricting crib that Mommy still won't get rid of and padded across the floor to the back door. You want to know: Why does the sun wake up? So here you are, alone after an early morning rain.

Then you see it, just above the horizon: the sun. It glows serenely in the pale mist – a small sliver. You wonder, how come it is so small? Breaking the silence, the back door slides open behind you. Your eyes turn away from the sky and land on Mommy. She is dressed in her purple pyjamas with the hearts and her hands are wrapped around herself.

"Honey, why are you out here all alone? Aren't you cold? It's not time to get up yet," she says and smiles at you.

"Buttttt… the sun's waking up. And I'm not cold Mommy – I have Lily!" You hold up your fairy doll. The one with the pink dress made of curling petals. The one that you sleep with every night.

"Of course, sweetie. Oh –" She looks up and sees the sun waking up. You knew she would like it. Mommy always likes magical things like that. You stand together, watching the red

Dawn

sun spring from the earth, climbing higher and higher into the blue, pushing mist out of its way. Finally, it is full and smiling in front of you.

"Mommy, why does the sun wake up like that? Why does it glow so reddish?" you wonder aloud.

Well," she starts, and pauses, looking down at you and Lily, "when the sun is gone, it's in the fairy world."

You look up at her, in awe. Mommy knows everything.

"What next, what next," you shriek.

"Shh, let me tell the story. When the fairies are going to sleep, they have to get the sun out of their world – it's just too bright to sleep with the lights on." She looks happy, so you nod encouragingly: "So all the fairies bring their wands and launch into the air, bringing the sun with them. Higher and higher, they're pulling the sun with their magic. Until..." she looks like she's about to go back inside.

"Don't, Mommy! Finish the story! Pleeeeease," you try to look cute, but end up making a monster face. Mommy laughs.

"Okay, okay, settle down. When the fairies reach the human world, their wands are running out of magic! So they use all the magic they have left, and send the sun, glowing deep red, into our sky. Then they fly back to their home. Anyway... it's cold out. C'mon honey, let's go back inside," she motions for you to come, and holds out her hand.

"Thank you for the story, Mommy," you say as you turn, one last time. You stare at the sun and swear that you see the magic dancing around it, and a cluster of fairies, flying down into the mist.

* * * * *

You walk into your classroom and sit down on the carpet. Today, your class is learning about space and you are so excited! It is your absolute, most favourite thing! You don't know much about it, but you sure love lying down in the backyard and staring at the stars. The kids around you are sitting down. It was cold at recess, and most of them have rosy cheeks and messy hair. Your teacher gets up from her desk and sits in the big chair beside the whiteboard at the front of the carpet. Your teacher is so nice – almost as nice as your Mom!

"Class, recess is over! Stop chit-chatting with your neighbours!"

Everyone stops talking, like your teacher pressed a magic BE QUIET button.

"Thank you," the teacher says. "Today we're talking about our solar system. Does anyone know how many planets there are? Yes?"

"Nine!" says someone from the back of the carpet.

"Actually, there are only eight planets," says your teacher. "Their names are Mercury, Venus, Earth, Mars, Jupiter, Saturn, Uranus, and Neptune." Your teacher draws them out in order on the whiteboard – the ones at the end are giant!

"What about Pluto?" someone calls out. The teacher looks across the room for the offender, and speaks:

"Class, raise your hand if you have a question. Anyway, Pluto isn't considered to be a planet anymore – it's too small! So now, does anyone know why the sun rises and sets?"

I do, you think, the fairies are pushing the sun with their magic! You smile contentedly.

"No one? Well, it's because the Earth is rotating around the sun!" Your teacher draws it on the whiteboard. You look up confused. "So the sun doesn't actually move. It just appears to be, since the Earth is rotating!" Two of your classmates go up to the front, and your teacher helps them demonstrate with a flashlight.

Mom lied, you think. Mommy – why? Why would you lie to me? Your thoughts swirl rapidly in your mind, trying to escape. You can't believe it. Mommy… No. NO!

Dawn

* * * * *

You are standing outside, waiting for the sunrise. Like you have done countless times over the years, leaning against the railing. You're tense. Lily, your worn and tearing doll, hangs limply from your hand. The sun starts to appear above the horizon, appearing as a sliver to a half to a whole. You look for the glow – the magic, but there's nothing.

All you can think of is the Earth turning in space and the sun staying still. Its not being pushed. You cannot see the fairies. There are none. Lily drops from your hand as you walk slowly back into the house and sit down, staring. The kitchen table is a blur. Everything is dripping. Like raindrops, but salty and full of pain.

Mommy, why would you lie? I TRUSTED you. I trusted you…

You stare blankly into the blur as teardrops slide down your face. You hear footsteps, and see a blurry purple figure step into the kitchen. You turn toward the wall.

"Honey, are you okay? What happened?" she asks, sleepy and concerned.

"You," you whisper to Mommy. Your voice cracks.

"Me?"

"You lied."

"About what?" She takes a tissue and wipes the tears from your eyes. She brings up a chair and sits in front of you.

"About the fairies, you lied, they're fake. I… I trusted you!" Your mind spins in a frenzy of betrayal.

"Oh."

She reaches up and pulls a strand of hair from her eyes. You look at the cold tile floor and trace the lines with your gaze. Your face still feels wet, and sadness engulfs the room. Mommy doesn't say anything.

Silence.

"Well, I was just telling you the story that my mother told me when I was young." She reaches out her hand, but you pull away.

"So where are the fairies?" you ask, with tears falling and blurring once more. "Do you believe in them?"

Mommy brings her chair closer. You look up and wipe your eyes with the sleeve of her purple pyjamas. The ones with the hearts.

"So?" You turn toward her.

"They're in here," she points to your chest, "in our hearts."

She gives you a hug. And you know, in that moment, that magic is real.

RUNNER UP

Scorched

Morgan Curtis

All I remember is the fire. The heat. The red flames eating away at my flesh. Everything else is blank, wiped from existence. The fire felt as if it had a hunger that could only be satisfied after everything that I am had been consumed. But I am alive. How am I alive? I should be nothing but a pile of ash, being blown away by the wind. But there is no wind.

There is no colour for as far as my eyes can see. The only colour is me. It is not dark, everything is just the same deep black. I can see the ground, the black ground. I see the black sky, the black trees, grass, flowers, and the black trail ahead of me. I look around in confusion, I feel like I should be scared, but I'm not. I only feel confusion. I have no memories, I do not remember having a family or friends. I know basic things like how to read, write, speak, and ride a bike, I just don't remember doing any of them.

I look at the sky, amused at its unusual colour, and see something that only furthers my confusion. It is all alone in the sky, a cloud the colour of blood. I've seen the colour before, I could never forget this colour, it's the colour of the fire. The red fire I thought killed me. The fire that didn't kill me. The fire that should've killed me. I look away from the red cloud in the black sky, but when I lower my head, everything is gone, the trees, the flowers. All that remains is the cloud. The scarlet red cloud in the charcoal black sky.

I can no longer contain my curiosity, it takes over my body, causing me to take a careful yet confident step forward. I wait. Nothing. I keep walking, but still nothing happens. I stop and look up at the cloud again. It seems larger, closer, redder. Now the cloud looks about twenty, maybe fifteen feet above my head. I take half a step backward and almost fall. The ground is gone, except for a circular platform I'm currently standing on. The cloud isn't coming toward me, the ground is lifting me to the cloud. I can't keep walking because I'll plummet to the ground. So I just sit on the platform and wait. I don't understand any of this. Nothing that is happening to me makes any sense. I start thinking and realize, I don't know who I am. I take a long look at myself. I don't know my name, my eye colour, my age, or even my gender.

After a few minutes of sitting in silence, the cloud is close enough for me to reach. I hesitantly move my hand up to touch it. Right as the tips of my fingers touch the cloud, I feel a scorching pain. I jerk my hand away, grunting in pain. The pain doesn't stay in my finger tips for long. Within seconds it is travelling throughout my entire body, searing my flesh. The pain feels familiar, it feels like the fire. It's happening again. The same pain is killing me all over again. But I won't die. I would rather die than go through this pain again. The pain is gone within seconds. It's gone like it was never there. All that pain, just vanished.

My eyes are closed, afraid of what they will see. I open them with caution. The black is gone, all of it. I am not even in the same place. I am in a room that is made entirely out of metal. I look around, confused by how I got here. There are no doors or windows. The room is empty except for a desk in the corner.

The floor is cold against my feet as a walk towards the desk. The desk has three drawers, one with a lock on it, two without. My shuddering, blood-covered hand pulls the cool metal han-

Scorched

dle of the top drawer, which has no lock. It's empty. I open the middle drawer. At first I don't see it, but I pull the drawer farther and see a pen, stapler, and paperclip in the back. I take each of them out and place them on top of the desk. I pull on the handle of the locked drawer, it does not move. I take the paperclip from the desk and unfold it to unlock the drawer. I stick both ends of it inside the keyhole, and somehow I know the correct way to pick locks, because it opens right away.

Inside the drawer there is a paper file that has the words, "Here Lies The Truth," written on it. I open it slowly. There is a single sheet of paper inside that has someone's personal information and records. I read the paper carefully, looking for anything important that could help explain what is happening to me.

> Name: Jude Abel
> Age: 18
> Gender: Other
> Date of birth: January 1, 2100
> Father: Unknown
> Mother: Unknown
> Species: Unknown

I don't understand, who is this about? Is this me, is all this information mine? If it is, I don't make much sense. What am I if not human? Who are my parents? What is my gender? The only thing I know, (if this paper actually is about me) is that my name is Jude, I was born on the first of January, 2100, and the year is either 2118 or later. I flip the paper and continue to read.

> Convicted of: Theft, refusing compliance, and causing war among the Clans of Authority
> Date of Imprisonment: May 24, 2114
> Date of Escape: September 3, 2116

What? I think. Convicted of causing war among the Clans of Authority? What does that mean? If I did all of this, which I assume I did, how could I have caused a war? Was I a fugitive? I must have been. Maybe that is why I'm here. Maybe wiping my memory and burning me alive is my punishment for everything I did wrong.

I put the paper back into the file and go to put it back in the drawer. As I am pulling the handle, I see something in the drawer that was not there before. There is a mirror, laying on top of it is a picture of someone. I take the picture in one hand and the mirror in the other.

I'm scared to look in the mirror and see the person looking back at me. I slowly and hesitantly raise the mirror so that it is level with my face. I look at myself in the mirror. I look back at the picture. The picture is of me. But I was much younger in this picture, much cleaner. I take a closer look at myself in the mirror. My face is covered in smeared dirt and blood, and my eyes look tired and sad, as if all happiness has been sucked from them. My hair is down to my shoulders and has too many knots to count. I put the mirror back into the drawer and look at the picture. I flip the picture and on the back it says, "Jude". The file is about me. I am a fugitive. I started a war. I am not human.

Suddenly, the room becomes dark, and I hear banging on the walls. I crawl underneath the desk and shove the picture between my hip and my pants. Within seconds the banging stops, and all I hear is the sound of my own breath. I stay under the desk, waiting for something to happen. Maybe whoever put me here is coming back to punish me again.

The room becomes light again and I crawl out from under the desk and stand up. I see something in the corner of my eye and turn my head to the left. There are three words written on the wall –

"We Are Coming."

GRADES 7 - 8

1st PLACE

Titles in Motion

Julia Llewellyn

Some people would call this "motivational". Some would call it "work". Some would call it "a waste of time". It's my life, and it's pretty much this: wake up in the morning, check the clock, check my schedule, press the informer to let my mom know I'm awake, and start my day. My day can be three things; I can go to school, to a court session, or to any volunteering shelter. In each and every case, it's so that I'm able to help people. That's all I do. Everyone is always congratulating me and thanking me for volunteering. More like being "volun-told". My mother signs me up for these things. "It's for a good cause Erica." I wish I could change this somehow, but my mom has my life pretty much planned out for me. I'm surprised that she hasn't picked out a spouse for me. I'm positive she will in the future.

    I click on the informer. I'm awake. The informer is a little device that my father invented. That's what he does for a living. We're kind of just testing it out. It's about the size of a kitchen timer, with two buttons on it. One is red, and the other is green. Green means "on time", and red, as you've probably assumed, means "late". My mother and father's lives are all about schedules. Meetings here, book signings there, "Don't forget to pick up Erica from her community service." Erica; that's me. "The One Who Helps". That's my title.

    I like titles. I believe everyone has one. Some are better than others, but we all have them. My mother's is "The One

Who Cares". That's how everybody thinks of her. She donates, and sponsors, and volunteers. But she doesn't really care. All she cares about is dates, times, and money. And then there's my father. He is "The One Who Creates". That's all he does. Day and night. He even created me. Bad joke.

I climb out of my bed, and soon after, make it. I pull off my nightdress and put on the outfit I picked out yesterday, which consists of a bra, panties, a pair of jeans, and one of my worn-out, black, oversized tee-shirts. I tie the shirt behind my back with an elastic and push the part that hangs out up underneath my shirt so it doesn't hang down. My midriff is showing below my shirt, and above the low-wasted jeans. My mother would disapprove. She's not home right now.

I step out of my room, and walk down the hall towards the washroom. Once I'm inside, I shut the door and lock it. I do my business, and wash my hands. As I turn off the tap, I look at myself in the mirror. I examine my eyes, my cheekbones, my eyebrows, my eyelashes. My lips are cracking and dry. I dry my hands on the towel and turn back to the mirror again. I grab my brush and smooth out my hair. I get rid of all the knots and shake my hair out. It falls back down around my shoulders, in a long, brown, glossy curtain, surrounding my face, and reaching my butt. It's as wavy as normal. I throw it up into a ponytail and leave the bathroom without looking in the mirror again.

"Good morning Erica," my father says without lifting his eyes from the piece of machinery that he's working on this morning.

"Good morning Father. Toast this morning?" I ask him, already knowing his answer. It's part of the schedule, but I still ask every morning.

"Yes Erica. Brown bread and jelly," he answers, like normal. I pull out my book of titles from the shelf where all of the cookbooks sit. Then I pop a slice of brown bread in the toaster. I write the date, and write, "Father: ✓". He is still "The One Who Creates". I always look for a change in his title, but like most titles, his never changes. Next I write "Mother:" knowing she will be my next interaction today.

Some kids have diaries or journals; I have a *Book of Titles*. Every person I meet has a title. Every person I interact with gets written down on the day we interacted, along with either a "✓" or a new title. There is rarely a new title these days. I can't help but judge a book by its cover; or a person by his/her first words.

My toast pops from the toaster. I put it on a plate, smother it with jelly, and sit down at the table with it. I flip back one page and read the entries from the previous day of title entries. I scan through all of the names. Beside each one is a check. Everyone is too predictable. This is something I don't want to be. But at the end of every day, my title stays the same: "The One Who Helps".

I take a bite of my toast. I don't bother trying to talk to my dad. He's too busy. As usual. Like everyone else. I wonder who I'll meet today. That's one upside to volunteering: I get to meet new people; people who aren't as predictable. Sadly, I most likely will never see them again. There's another thing about me…I don't have friends. I'm sure it's because of my personality. I'm too judgy. I just can't help it. My titles are my life. They're what I get up every morning for. I wake up on time, arrive at shelters or school on time, to discover new titles. To meet new people. When I meet a new person, I pull out my book and write down their name, and their title. Everyone's always weirded out about it. Nobody accepts it.

I take another bite of my toast. I don't need someone predictable. I don't need friends. I'm fine on my own.

I hear the front door open. I sit up straighter and pull my shirt down farther. The door closes and keys jingle as they're hung by the door. My mother enters the kitchen. I give her a small smile. Hope. Will she have changed?

"Erica, you're going to the shelter this morning. You're going to help the poor animals," my mother announces. She pauses to smile, "Good morning Fredrick." I sigh and my smile fades. "✓".

"Good morning dear. I think I may have figured out how to make a portable informer. Using the telephone lines of course," my father tells her.

"Lovely. Erica, hurry up and finish your toast or you'll be late," she demands.

"Yes mother," I say and give her a small smile. She looks down on me over her nose and nods. Approved.

"Good girl. Frederick, we have a meeting with Miss Elinor today at noon. Be there. This may be your golden opportunity to show her and the company the informer," my mother demands. She demands a lot.

"Yes dear," he says and goes back to work.

I finish my toast and wash off my plate. Then I meet my mother at the door and slip my shoes on.

"Come Erica. You're going to be late," my mother says. Of course I'm not going to be late, but I do as I'm told. We walk out to the car and I slip in shotgun. Then I pick up my *Book of Titles* from my lap.

"Erica, what's that?" my mother asks looking at it. I'm surprised she even noticed.

"It's my *Book of Titles* mother. It's something I've been working on for–" I realize I have her full attention. Maybe for the first time in my life she's really interested, eye contact and all, "– two years. I have more than one book, but this is my current one–"

"Erica, you're babbling. And sit up straight, you're slouching," my mother says. The smile that was on my face vanishes. I turn away and look out the window.

"Chin up! Smile! You're helping people!" my mother says enthusiastically, waving at a passing jogger and smiling. I turn and face the windshield obediently. I raise my chin and plaster a fake smile across my face. My mother starts the car. And we're off to the shelter. Yet another day of my being, "The One Who Helps". But I guess that's all I'll ever be. I'm just putting my title in motion.

"Erica: ✓"

2nd PLACE

Unexplained

Aluki Chupik-Hall

Alexander never liked himself. He was made up of anxious thoughts; the shy boy who always pretended he was having fun, but never really was. He thought he was ugly. On the outside he was average, long black unkempt hair that fell, uncaring, around his shoulders. A small round face, freckles spilled across it like stars. Wide eyes, curious, innocent. Even under all that he was ugly. He thought destructive thoughts and had bursts of anger that were too strange for society. He was bizarre, swimming in a vast ocean of normal.

And then there was Raven. He was all the colours, thrown around on a canvas carelessly to make something beautiful. He had curly orange-tinted hair, bouncing every step, sad eyes that never seemed sad. He was tall, and under that he was amazing. People said he was a prodigy in the art world, his pieces selling for thousands or sometimes millions in galleries around the globe. He was perfect, and Alexander was broken, and they lived next door to each other.

Alexander had always wanted to be an artist since he was small. He never had the patience, and would destroy his work in flashes of horrible red, uncontainable rage, but Raven had the patience of a grand oak tree, standing strong in a calm, green forest for hundreds of years. They often found refuge hidden away in Raven's studio, a small room with canvases scattered across the floor in a way that you could barely take a step. The air was thick with the chemical smell of colourful paints. Alexander found it funny how million-dollar paintings could be thrown to the floor so carelessly, and it bothered him greatly. One day Alexander was sitting across from him as he painted. Watching, wondering silently, how?

"I don't understand you," Alexander said, edges of frustration in his voice.

Raven merely smiled. "I don't understand myself half the time either. There are just some things we must leave unknown and unexplained." Raven continued to paint.

Alexander grunted. He didn't entirely agree, but Raven was smart. That was another thing. He had just the right elements of wise and completely insane. Purples and oranges. Harmony. Balance.

"That's not right." The anger in Alexander's voice thickened. "There's an explanation for everything! I thought you were smart, you should know that!"

Pink to red. Raven pushed the wooden edge of his paintbrush to his chin, his brow furrowed in thought as he stared at the painting. His eyes darted madly across the canvas, scanning every detail. He brought the brush to the paper.

"Oh, things always have explanations," Raven said, thoughtfully. "Sometimes it's just best not to hear them."

Alexander tensed, standing. "No." He began to breathe heavily. "It's wrong not to explain things. It leaves people uneasy."

Raven stood to match Alexander. "I'm sorry," he said.

Alexander softened at the unpredictable response.

"I know what it's like to be..." Raven searched for the word, taking a lingering second to find it. "...unexplained."

Alexander bit his lip. Raven wasn't as perfect as Alexander thought. But he didn't know the struggle. Not like he did. He sat back down, tired of arguing. Raven stayed standing for a moment, as if the conversation was unfinished. Looking around awkwardly, he sat down to finish the painting. Alexander watched him in wonder, his fire cooling. Blue. But a sharp blue. Alexander never had colours without them being loud, bright. Everything was turned to the highest volume, everything was overwhelming.

Raven spoke. "You know, Alexander, it's more than alright to be different." He smiled.

"No," Alexander replied, the question repeating itself in his head, taking a moment to become clear. "Not my kind of different."

Raven nodded, his grin fading.

Something told Alexander that Raven knew more than he thought he did.

"But it's pure pain to never have an explanation. It's worse to be like us," Raven said. He closed his eyes for a moment.

"I'm not like you." Alexander shook his head.

"Why not?"

"Because you have purpose. Your different was made for something, and so people accept it. You aren't just a strange little boy, lying in the defect pile. You aren't different, you're special." Alexander felt a wave of emotions come over him. All the colours in a thick, nauseating soup.

Raven took a moment before he spoke. "They didn't always say that." He closed his eyes again to prevent a few tears from escaping. He was all the colours, passing through his head in electric bursts of chaos. A million things to say, but only few that he knew he was allowed to. He had to watch for people's reactions, make sure what he said was normal. He had to chose, he had to separate. Maybe everyone was their own kind of different. Maybe the world of strangers around them had their own colours to hide. Raven wasn't perfect. He was hiding. He had built a barrier of perfection. But it wasn't real, it wasn't Raven. Raven was an illusion, a trick to fool passers-by. They saw the barrier and moved on. After all, no one can see past illusions the first time. It took practice.

And that was what Alexander had. He knew how to read, but yet he did not know how to write. He didn't know how to build his own barrier.

"Maybe they were, in a way," Alexander replied, avoiding eye contact.

"How so?"

"Maybe they were jealous that you were different and they just…" Alexander paused.

"They just never needed to be explained," Raven finished. "And also, you said 'were', 'were different'. I still am. Just because I don't always seem so."

"Sometimes, it gives me the illusion…" Alexander started.

Raven stopped him. "I know." He took his brush off the paper. "I don't know why I have to hide, because I shouldn't."

"What were you painting?" Alexander peeked at his drawing.

"You," Raven said bluntly.

Alexander stared, wide eyed and flustered at his own face drawn across the canvas. It was so perfect, so tenderly done. Every detail. Every flaw. From this angle he almost looked normal. Nobody could tell who he was, what he had done. A strange feeling came over him. Like he wasn't so different after all. An earthy brown. The smell after a heavy rainfall. There were no bright neon colours, only the comforting shade.

"Why?" he asked, overwhelmed, but not in the usual way.

"Because I thought if you saw yourself from the outside then you might realise how normal different actually looks." Raven grinned proudly.

Alexander returned his smile. He was right.

3rd PLACE

My Name is Mapiya

Maeve Brennagh Mackie

Mami always told me that my name meant the sky, that I was a free spirit. The sky doesn't belong in a cage, though. Mami always told me as she braided my long hair that she would never let me go. Now my hair is gone and she let them take me away. How could she break her promises? I used to want to go home, but now it seems I don't belong anywhere.

The Governess is coming. I can hear her clearly in the next room down, roaring like a bear. Pushing little girls off their cots, she threatens them. She'll not give them breakfast. She'll whip them hard. But those are the newcomers. In my room, we're all accustomed to this hellish place.

I've been here for so many moons that I can't even remember what it was like in my village. Eyota can, though. She came from a village near mine around the same time I did. Eyota is so darn stubborn that sometimes she even speaks Forbidden when the Fathers aren't around. Chatan and I, we tell her that she'll get a good whipping, but Eyota doesn't care.

"Up, up, UP!" Governess screams, sending her spit flying all over us. I hop to my feet, and scramble to tug the potato sack dress over my stubbly head. The dress is a hand-me-down, infested with grime, sweat, and bedbugs. Chatan says that the white people put their diseases in the sacks, but that's just a silly rumour. Even though it's filthy, this garment is all that I own. I don't have a toothbrush, a comb, or even a pillow.

Just like every morning, we march in a ruler straight line behind Governess' many bustling skirts to the dining hall. The hall is really just a big wooden barn that is slowly caving in.

This morning is the same as every other day's breakfast: strange beige mush with some stray flies in it and muddy water. The Fathers call the mush "pablum", whatever that means. All I notice is how utterly disgusting it is. Chatan says that Cook gets the water from the school's sewers. I wouldn't be surprised if this were true!

Today is a Sunday, so we must gather for chapel outside. The Fathers call it "chapel" anyways, but my friends and I know that it's really drills. We must repeat verses from the Bible for many hours. The Bible is a thick book that the Christian white men use to teach us. Why would you need a book when you could just tell interesting stories like Mami did? If we do not pronounce the words correctly or repeat in unison, that means an after dinner whipping. All the Fathers gather in the dining hall to watch tiny children suffer. I cannot imagine what could possibly be crueler.

On the way back from chapel, I spot my brother. It has been so long since I saw his last that I can't even remember his name. Memories rush back to me as I stare into his tired face.

Playing happily by the river while our mother hung clothes to dry. Crawling into Mami's lap to hear her stories, shivering and damp. Falling asleep while she spun wonderful tales of the animals, the people, and the land. Rocking us back and forth, back and forth. Whispering to us: Thečhíȟila, *I love you.*

The day the men came and took us away. My brother screaming as we left, his throat hoarse. Mami's face stained with oceans of tears, weeping like she never had before; held back as she tried to get to us. And then she was gone. Our lives stolen.

But I cannot shout out to him, for fear of being noticed. It is much safer to blend into the background. He wouldn't

My Name is Mapiya
A Residential School Story

respond anyways, his scars have silenced him.

I trudge back through the barren, rain-soaked fields for lunch. Usually, I skip lunch though. I'd much rather be starving than sick. Lunch is followed by a class. Iron desks bolted into the floor and stained walls in every room. There is a corner to stand in for speaking Forbidden and a ruler that Teacher raps your knuckles with until they are raw and bleeding.

They call this place "a school where the Savages can learn." The Teachers cleaned up once so photographers could take fake photographs to prove that we are learning. But is a school really a place where children are wiped of their identity? Is it a place where we are herded like sheep? Should Eyota and I cry ourselves to sleep each night?

"I brought you some bread," whispers a meagre voice, and a warm object is pushed into my hand. Astonished, I look up and wipe the salty tears off my face. Standing in front of me is my brother.

"Oh, Mapiya," he sobs. As we wrap our arms around each other, I realize that maybe I could give Mami another chance. Maybe I could give hope a chance, too. My brother reaches out for my hand, and I squeeze it tight.

RUNNER UP

Luna

Luiza Aguilar

It's funny. Only when things are totally gone do we really understand them. Only when I lost you did we become united forever. It doesn't make sense, of course, but logic and sense should be left to the imagination; life is already full enough of confusion. When you were with me, I knew only what you showed me. But now, I see all of you. Perhaps you don't know what I'm talking about. I'll tell you the story.

It all happened that winter day. You wouldn't recognize the one, so I'll describe it for you. It really was a lovely day, at least as long as the arms of morning held time in their comfort. Despite the clouds, the sun glowed, lining the skies in that radiant golden colour that makes even the most unaffected spirits crave something more. The icy tips of lonely branches glimmered in the dazzling, radiant light, reminding the universe that beauty hadn't completely disappeared. Even the fresh layer of snow beneath our feet seemed to glister. The day seemed too beautiful for the cunning, slender fingers of Tragedy to touch it, but now, I see that's why they decided to reach in the first place.

The start to the day was so familiar, it could have, in anyone else's mind, brazed to the days preceding it. I woke to an ignorance in my mind so obtuse I couldn't even recognize it for what it was. I went through my morning routine in the most typical way, a way without room for thought or reflection, as if I was but a leaf drifting mindlessly in the icy breeze.

This monotonous pattern went on into the start of the afternoon, I think.

My phone rang, but since the number wasn't one in my address book, I opted not to answer. When it rang again and the same number came up once more, I declined again. The third time, I just couldn't handle the caller's utter lack of civility. And so, I blocked the number, not realizing I was making one of the greatest mistakes of my life.

A few minutes went by, and I forgot about the phone call, as one does in times of most unawareness. It was just another moment of my day, one inconsequential puzzle piece in hundreds. I think we realize too late that a single missing piece can so easily destroy a whole puzzle.

Suddenly, my phone rang again. I must have been a bit irritable after the events moments before, because the sort of wave of easy release that always washed over me at the sight of your name in my phone drowned me, and I answered the call as hostile as a storm, and as forceful.

"Luna," I said. "I'm really busy, is this…" I cut myself short at the sound of hushed voices and loud beeping.

"Grant," you said. I felt the pain in your voice; it almost shattered me. "Why weren't you answering your phone?"

In that moment, I put it all together. The unfamiliar number. The beeping. The struggling.

"What happened?" I asked, but I already knew.

"It's back," you said, and took in a sharp breath. "They think the cancer's back."

And right then, in the middle of the sidewalk, I crumbled down to my knees in despair, my phone landing a few feet away. People whipped past me, each one as insignificant as a fly, and as hopelessly irritating. The entire universe seemed to shrink in that moment, caving in on me as every piece of my being unravelled into nothing.

I felt trapped in the depths of human suffering, enclosed in the uninhabitable hotel of my own life, where I'd be bound until my spirit found the strength to travel elsewhere. And the worst thing was, I'd not even another poisoned soul to keep me company. And you, Luna, you were millions of miles away, hanging like a marionette in the sky.

I forgot you were still on the phone somewhere expecting a response, so I just lay, contemplating the unfairness of the universe. Some part of me heard you tell me they were only running tests, that everything might be okay. Somewhere, I knew you were asking me to visit you, telling me not to get worked up, that they said it might just be some kind of pneumonia. Tragedy held me in a place where the only things I saw, the only things I heard, were the sounds of my own anguish. The only thing that stirred me, finally, was the sound of the call ending a while later.

I was so angry then, at the universe and at you; yet somehow not at Tragedy, the one who had pressed the button to end our connection. I mistook her cruel sneers for the sound of my own regretful submission, and for the sound of the universe taunting me, urging me to give up. But I wouldn't; I needed to see you.

I sat in the passenger seat in a mad, passionate daze as Tragedy drove me straight to the hospital, the shadow of a smirk on her face.

We turned the final corner, and I saw the hospital up ahead, urging me forward, yet warning me of something. A moment too late, I figured out what.

As I made the turn, a pristine-looking car of a scarlet colour, matching Tragedy's silk gown, pulled out of a driveway. In half a fleeting moment, we collided, and I became Tragedy. My eyes glistened with the glow of her subtle depravity, and for that moment, I understood what made evil so marvellous and devilry so alluring. I can't remember what made me understand, or what I understood, but for those final moments, it all made sense. It might have been fantastic; that feeling of understanding.

But through it all, I thought only of you and the worry devouring me from the inside. My last thoughts before everything disappeared were not of wickedness, but of sorrow.

When I woke up, the universe had disguised itself with the fog of uncertainty, hiding behind unanswered questions and lost moments. A blurry face told me I'd been in a coma, and my memory was failing, whatever that meant. I spent many suns in a pale blue room, with only shadowy figures to keep me company.

Each day when I woke up, I'd meet the room again for the first time, and each night, I'd fall asleep thinking I never had before. I never got past the first times. Through it all, you offered me companionship, at least in my mind. You were the sun I could see even through a foggy pane of glass.

I started seeing a specialist – at least he tells me I did. I can't seem to recollect seeing him at all. He told me I had a memory condition. He asked whether I remembered anything at all; I'd lost all that could tell him who I was, he told me.

So, I told him about you, about us. I told him everything. And he listened, pausing once in a while to write something down or to remind me what I was talking about when it slips away. He asked if I knew how to find you, and I told him to check for you in the hospital. But you weren't there.

It's funny. Like everything else in my life, you left without even footprints to lead me to you. We're separated by a distance that can't be measured in miles. If you weren't holding on so tightly to what's left of my memory, I might believe you were just a shadow.

But you're so vivid in my mind. It's like you're a part of me. The only missing piece is your name; you weren't really called

Luna, but when I couldn't remember who you really were, I started calling you that. It reminds me of you.

I'll never understand how my memories of you are as clear as my own reflection, when the whole universe is a distorted image a million miles away. You're so absent outside of my mind, yet so present in it.

I'm starting to wonder if that's where you've always been.

RUNNER UP
Alex Von Valentine
Victoria Casey

Hello there readers... No, that sounds stupid... How about, Hey... No, no, that's not any better... Um... You know what? I can't think of a good intro so how about I just tell you who I am? That's probably better.

My name is Alex Von Valentine. I know, I sound like a supervillain from the cheesiest superhero movie. Although that would be awesome, that's not the case. I am just a fifteen year old girl going to Scarlet Rose Petal High School. I take English and Math, and all the boring subjects. Not at will, of course. I'm only in ninth grade so I don't get to pick my subjects.

Because you obviously can't see me... I'm going to tell you what I look like. I look like a magical princess... Haha, just kidding. I have jet black long hair and black glasses. My pale skin really brings out the colour. I usually wear my white tank top with a black cardigan and jeans. And black combat boots. I know what you're thinking – "this girl is awesome" – but trust me, I'm not; or at least the people in my school don't think so. Now... let me tell you my fabulous story... DOM DOM DOM DOM!...

I grew up like a regular kid. Barbies, princesses and mud. I have amazing parents. My mom's name is Sunshine Valentine. She's a very famous makeup artist. She does many tutorials on youtube, and sometimes even models and movies. My Dad is Micah Valentine. He's the head boss person for Blount

Canada. He owns all of them. I live in the small but charming, Guelph, Ontario. I grew up here. I know how to walk to everywhere in the city.

As kids go, you could say that I'm more awesome than all others, not to brag… I am a total nerd. I asked my friend Waverley who was her favourite Avenger and she asked, "What's the Avengers?" I almost lost it; almost made her sit down and watch it.

Anyway, more to the point, I'm not popular; I'm more of a wallflower, not really starting anything, etc. But the other day… all of that changed. I was just leaving the school when I saw these grade ten boys bullying a grade nine boy… I don't know why, I guess because he was such a nerd. I wasn't having a great day and I was a little angry, I have to admit, so I did something I wouldn't normally do. Instead of staying out of it, I marched right over there to protect my fellow nerd. Heroic, I know.

"Get your hands off of him!" I yelled.

"Get lost, whatever your name is," one of the boys yelled.

I was now walking toward them as they were backing up, "Who do you think you are?! It's three against one, and he did nothing wrong!" I yelled.

The boys backed up looking angry.

"Who gave you the right to think of yourself as better than him?" I continued.

"And who are you?" one of the boys stupidly asked.

"A person! And so is he!" I said angrily.

"Eh… ye – yes. I just…" The boys hit a tree and stumbled backward.

"Just what? Thought you could just waltz in here like you're better than everyone? Newsflash buddy! You're not! We're all equal whether you like it or not!"

The boys walked away with attitude.

I turned around. "Are you okay?" I asked the boy.

"I'm fine. Thank you, Alex," he said.

"How did you know my name?" I asked.

"Us nerds need to stick together." He winked and walked away.

I went home feeling confident, and proud! The next day I walked into the halls of my school. Everyone stopped, stared and parted as I walked. I was confused. People usually just pretend I'm not there. People whispered and gossipped. I went to Waverley, and she looked worried. Her long green hair was tucked behind her ears, which usually means something's up.

"Whats going on?" I asked.

"Yesterday, some kid got your courageous fight on video and posted it to youtube. They also sent it to everyone in the school titled, 'Everyday Hero'. You made the bullies of the school run, and that *never* happens!" She said excitedly.

Many teachers stopped me that day to congratulate me. I don't know what I did that was so spectacular. It's sad that this is something so bad that we have to congratulate the few people who stop it. We had an assembly that day, The principal gave me the "Stand up to bullying award". I'm fairly certain he just made that up, but whatever, I was honoured. I wasn't a nobody anymore. My life was changed for the better. More and more people started standing up for themselves. The bullying rate at our school dropped to practically zero. And all it took was one person. One person who stood up for somebody, and did something good. I, Alex von Valentine, actually helped, even if it was just one person, it changed everything. All for the better…

RUNNER UP

The Vaccine

Grace Ma

The scientist leaned back in her chair, a smile plastered on her face. She clapped her hands together and stretched her arms. The formula was complete.

Her hand reached up and grabbed the letter she was writing to her mother.

"Today is a good day," she wrote. "The sky is a bright blue canvas. The clouds fingerprint-paint it and the illuminating sun shines on a stream. Today is a good day, and I have finished my work." The scientist scribbled a few more sentences, then she carefully sealed the envelope and got up to deliver it.

Suddenly, in the corner of her eye, something moved. She saw a silver object and curly brown hair. She reached for the piece of lined paper that held the world's fate. If this fell into the wrong hands, then everything she'd worked towards, her whole life would fall apart.

"I wouldn't rip that that if I were you," snarled a familiar voice.

Within seconds, all that remained in the lab was a shredded piece of paper, a letter and a body.

Red high heels struck the floor. The letter was taken. The shreds of paper were carefully collected.

"I'll deliver this to Mother for you."

It was a good day. The clouds fingerprinted the bright blue sky and the illuminating sun shone on a stream.

The Vaccine

The murderer was successful. And she would be, for a long time.

* * * * *

ONE HUNDRED YEARS LATER

I wipe my sweaty palms on my charcoal-grey shirt. Hanging from a door is a bright sign announcing in bold letters, "MANDATORY NEEDLE SHOTS TODAY!" that jumps out at me. I'm the last student in line for the needle shots – the rest of my classmates are waiting impatiently in the the hallway. A "reassuring" thumbs up from my teacher makes me even more nervous.

Ever since "The Murder", it was mandatory for every citizen at age thirteen to get a vaccine shot. Apparently, the shot is supposed to prevent all illnesses to the patient and a better chance of surviving trauma until the patient is fifty plus. I honestly have no idea how this works because I zone out every time someone explains it to me, but our territory has been doing it for one hundred years, so I guess it's working pretty well.

A door opens, making me jump. A stuck-up boy whose name I forget grins at me and confidently walks to the hallway. A woman in her twenties with a face caked with makeup smiles brightly at me, showing off her yellow crooked teeth.

"Come inside, dear. I'll be the one giving you your shot today. My name is…"

I zone out as she babbles on and on about safety concerns, terms and conditions and other useless information. I stare into space until the lights in the room flicker off and the room turns so dark, I can barely see my own hands. The woman trying to give me the vaccine curses, mutters something about a janitor and then smiles at me. She says something about being back in five minutes, and then quickly walks out of the room.

I go out to the hallway where the lights are still on. I inhale and exhale. Of course the power will go out when I'm getting a needle. My classmates are nowhere in sight – which is a bit odd, but I don't really care. I can't see my teacher, but I'm guessing that she forgot about me. It's not that hard, anyway I don't talk much, and I prefer to be alone.

Suddenly, the hot air coming from a vent shuts down. The lights in the hallway flicker and also shut down too. I can still see a dim light from the stairway, but after a few seconds the lights diminish.

I shiver and pull out my phone. The bright screen lights up for a second, but a low-battery warning quickly dismisses the light source.

I decide to walk around and look for the nurse who was supposed to be vaccinating me. After all, I think, the lights are off, the furnace is down, my phone is dead, and I have to get my vaccine eventually. What else can happen?

A note from the Future Me: This was not the best idea I have thought of.

I walk through the hallway and turn the corner. I'm a little freaked out, but I have the worst luck, so I'm not surprised that this is happening to me. Squish.

My foot lands in something warm. Liquid covers my sandal and I feel something faintly beating. My sandal gets stuck. My heart leaps to my throat. I feel something twitch, and then there's no more beating. The thing I'm stepping on spasms.

I open my mouth to scream, but someone grabs me from behind. I gasp as in one swift action something bitter is poured down my throat. There's a flash of light.

The nurse's dead body is the last thing I see before I fall to the ground. A note from the Future Me: I never even knew her name.

My eyes twitch. Everything feels numb, but I yawn and sit up. I rub my eyes and check my surroundings. I'm in my classroom everything looks normal, except there's a tiny flask on the floor next to me.

That's when everything flashes back. I sit there, shocked and shaking. I can't talk or even stand up.

"Impressive," says a voice. "She was only unconscious for ten minutes – that's a new record!"

"She's not asking questions either," says another voice.

"Be careful," a third voice says. "Quiet ones are dangerous."

I slowly look in the direction of the voices. Red hot anger rushes through me, replaces the fear and shock. I recognize them as my classmates Alison, Jack, and Caleb. I never really talked to them before, but they were always pulling pranks (or as they call it, "conducting experiments"). I heard that once they pretended to murder a girl. I stand up and walk towards the classroom door. I spin around and glare at them.

"Where'd you guys get that fake dead body? It was super cool." Then, I turn the door knob.

Something silver flashes in the corner of my eye. I see curly brown hair and red high heels. I remember reading something about this in history class, but I can't remember the details. I pause, and then slowly turn around.

"You're not really my classmates, are you? And I'm not really in my classroom, am I?"

Alison, Jack and Caleb have disappeared. In their place is a tall, skinny woman with curly brown hair, red lipstick and red high heels, holding a gun.

"Sit down," she says. "I'll tell you a story."

To be continued.

RUNNER UP

The Truth Behind the Flames

Grace Mitchell-Qahawish

I smelled the smoke before I saw the deep red flames.

I shrieked for Sandra and Ellie, and maybe even Lola. I heard a dog barking faintly and I ran towards it.

"LOLA?" I screamed. My bedroom door bursts into flames, the hot shadow of burning heat slowly coming towards me.

I heard Lola barking, and some yelling. I grabbed my bedside table water glass and threw it pathetically at the flames, as if a puddle of water would stop our house from burning down.

"I'm in here!" I yelled and spun around. I grabbed my fresh, light blue sheet from my dresser and threw half of it out my window. I held on to the soft cotton edge and tied the corner over my old bed frame pole.

I hurled myself out the window, holding onto my favourite bedsheet as tight as my hands let me. I slowly slid myself down my sheet, and a tear trickled down my cheek as I knew that would be the last time I saw my blue and green striped room.

Pathetic, crying over my bed sheets when I could be losing my family, right?

Maybe I was crying because I was scared. I knew my cat Jojo was already dead, because he's really stupid (sorry Jojo) and probably wanted to play with the flames.

At mum's bedroom window, I squeezed my sheet goodbye for the last time, lunged my body forwards to grab her balcony railing, and threw myself over it. Ouch. I landed on my stomach, and I was pretty sure I felt some blood running down my forehead.

"Come on, Kat!" I urged myself. Standing up, I scanned my mum's room. There was no one inside except –

"GRRR RUFF! AWOOOOOHF!"

"LOLA!" I ran to our black sheepoo, and hugged her.

As I squeezed her, I realized that she was VERY warm.

Oh. My. God.

"HELP! HELP ME!" I shrieked.

Fire started to break the ceiling, and it cracked, and just like that, my room fell onto my mum's bed.

Suddenly my eyes went dizzy, and all I could see was red, orange, and black fur that I had cradled against me. Lola was barking, and crying, panting for help.

I've lost my glasses. NO!

I tried to take deep breaths but my hand touched something HOT. Fire.

No point in looking for my glasses, wherever they were. I carefully felt around the room to my mum's window, and I twitched every time my foot touched a hot floor tile. I held my breath, whispered "I love you Lola," and jumped.

*****

I landed on something hard and cold.

I opened my eyes and ignored my pain. Against a dark, blurry sky I saw a black shape run towards me and jump on me.

"Lola!" I screamed with joy.

"Mum? Sandra? Ellie?" My body was trembling with fear. I forced myself onto my hands and knees, and rubbed my forehead.

Blood. Gross! I felt a pang of worry hit when I realized where I was. In the backyard, where no one could see me.

I scrambled forwards, but kept a tight grip on Lola's collar. I was NOT going to lose her again.

"KAT? KATHERINE?" Sandra?

"Baby girl, where are you?" Ellie!

"Sandy! Elles! I'm in the backyard!"

Then, thinking again:

"Girls? Are you okay? Where's mum?"

I saw two fuzzy figures run towards me, both with slim long legs. One was wearing a summer, knee-length light blue dress, the other wearing black leggings and a purple poncho.

Sandy and Ellie glanced at each other, and I don't have to have 20/20 vision to know that they're nervous about telling me. Something is wrong!

I started to panic. Is mum – dead?

No.

I burst into thick, heavy sobs, to the point where I couldn't move. Ellie stood beside me and wrapped me in her arms, and Sandy hugged us tight. Lola scampered over and hid under my legs.

Together, we watched our home go down in flames.

*****

"Well darlings, I should really get to bed. Please, feel free to make yourself at home to your heart's content!" Ms. Belle smiled warmly at each of us, and blew us kisses as she walked up her old fashioned stairs. SO not like my home. Everything was modern at my house.

Ms. Belle was our neighbor. She lived two houses down from my house, and was always the warmest woman on our street. She was a few years older than my mum.

We were forced to stay at her house until my mum got back from the hospital since Ms. Belle was her emergency contact. After the fire, Sandy called 911, and she had to sign a few forms. Apparently mum fell through the bathroom floor during my escape. John Meyer, our next door neighbor, heard the chaos and called 911. The ambulance came before me, Sandra, or Ellie had a chance to say goodbye. Mum broke a bone and had a few burns, but she was not too bad. I'll have to wait till I see her.

I glanced at Ellie, and she smiled nervously. We only had a week, just one week. 10:15 p.m....

At the dinner table, I shoved my plate with mashed potatoes and roasted chicken away. I wasn't hungry.

Sandy warned me. "Kat, don't be disrespectful of Ms. Belle! She's worked hard to make dinner for us, and the least you can do is appreciate it!" Sandra was a "sassy soldier", as we liked to call her. She was the oldest of us three sisters.

She sighed something about calling her boyfriend, Rob, washed her plate in the sink, and walked to her room.

Ellie mumbled, "I'm sorry this happened, Kat. I really am. This is all my fault. I'm a terrible person!"

"Oh. Elle! It's – it's – don't blame it on you! This isn't your fault! It could have happened to any of us!"

"I AM a bad person! What kind of person FORGETS TO TURN THE STOVE OFF!?"

I looked down to try and think of something to say. Somehow, my tongue found its sentence before my brain.

"Ellie, you're human! We should be grateful! Mum didn't die! We lost Jojo, but he was old! He's still in our hearts. For the sake of Mum, please, don't put the blame on yourself!"

She gave my hand a squeeze.

"Thanks Kat. You're the best."

I smiled.

* * * * *

"Well? Kat?" Chloe's curious blue eyes peered questioningly at me. "What do you think?" I glanced in the mirror and smiled. My new bright red glasses shimmered in the sun.

"They're perfect," Chloe agreed.

We walked out of the store and linked arms. Ms. Belle came up from behind us. I could finally see again! Wow!

"Well Chloe, I'd like to thank you personally for helping Katherine pick her glasses today. It's always easier when a best friend can help!"

We hopped into Ms. Belle's grey van, buckled our seatbelts, and sat quietly as Ms. Belle stepped on her rusty gas pedal.

I laughed, embarrassed. Chloe, my bestie snorted, as she always does when she's happy. I've known her since grade one. She had light brown hair that she always wore in a french braid to the side. Her high waisted shorts and floral crop top were in style.

She gave me a big hug.

"It was my pleasure, Ms. Belle!"

Me. Belle laughed. "Please, call me Selena! No need to be so formal!"

I opened my door when the car came to a sudden halt in front of the dirty white building.

Ms. Belle scrambled after me and pulled me to her ear. "Katherine, I just want you to know that you don't have to do this if you don't want to. I know you're anxious about it, darling," she whispered.

"Thanks, Selena, but – but – this is something I HAVE to do."

Selena nodded worriedly. "Alright then. We'll wait outside for you darling."

Chloe blew me a kiss, and I waved.

The Truth Behind the Flames

I walked through the hospital doors, and a lady in white clothing greeted me. She smiled warmly. "You're a brave girl."

I followed her until we got to the big glass hospital door, 184.

I shoved it open.

There she was, lying in bed. She turned her head slowly towards me, and her soft words echoed as she spoke.

"Katherine? Don't be afraid, dumpling. I'm okay."

I ran to her, and her scarred face managed to let out a radiant beautiful smile.

She opened her hands and I hugged her tight.

"I love you mum."

She started to cry lightly, but she breathed, "I love you too Katherine. I love you too."

RUNNER UP

Change is Constant

Emily Fritzley

The road is coarse, the clouds look mad, and the trees are rumbling everywhere. I'm so scared. It looks as if there's a bad storm coming on. Should mom and I be driving? Should we stop the car? As the last thought went through my head, bang, the car was hit.

Apparently, I'm in a hospital. "What happened?"

Mom just stares at me looking relieved.

"I can't feel anything from my waist down," I mutter softly. It's probably because I'm in shock; however the doctor should be in soon to tell me that everything is okay. At least I hope so, because I really want to get out of here soon. I have a big basketball game tonight.

The doctor walks in. She's talking quietly to my mom, so all I hear is that her name is Dr. Tomley blah… long recovery blah… and something else that I don't even understand. All I'm focusing on now is how to make sure I get to my game. My legs feel strange, but otherwise everything else feels completely normal until someone uses the word paralyzed. I'm really scared.

"Paralyzed? What do you mean paralyzed?"

"Yes," the doctor replies, "paralyzed, you're paralyzed from the waist down."

No, this can't be possible! Wait, this means I can't play basketball anymore; I can't do anything anymore! Why did this have to happen to me? I'm just a regular girl. On top of that,

I have to stay in the hospital for two weeks and sit in a dumb hospital bed, too.

The doctor tells me that she has set up an appointment tomorrow with the child life specialist at the hospital. Whatever that is! She says that I should make sure I see the specialist, because of all of my "frustrations". Why is a girl, whose life just changed forever, not allowed to be upset? It's pretty reasonable if you ask me.

Meanwhile, I'm heading to the other side of the hospital being pushed by a complete stranger! We're off to see the child life specialist. I hate the feeling of someone pushing me around in a wheelchair; it's like I can't do anything anymore!

I arrive at the child life specialist "room", I guess you could call it. Suddenly a mature, but a rather soft voice, says my name. "Hello, are you Reese?"

"Ummm, yeah, why do you ask?"

"My name is Lola, and I'm the Child Life Specialist at the hospital. I'm here to help you with anything that you may need and to answer any questions that you may have."

I couldn't care one bit who she was. My life was a mess and she couldn't help, so I said so. "Okay, but I still don't understand why I'm here. You couldn't help me even if you were the last person on earth!" I say angrily.

"Well, why don't you just come on in and we'll talk."

"If I have to."

'We're going to do an exercise that will relieve the stress and frustrations that you're having as you adjust to your new life."

"Whatever. This is all pointless anyway."

"Here's a syringe and a piece of paper. The syringe has paint in it. You're going to take it and squirt the paint from it onto the paper. As you're doing that, say something that you're upset about right now, something you wish you could forget."

"Wait up… you want me… to squirt paint… from a syringe… onto a piece of paper?!"

"Yes, I do."

"Wow, are you kidding me? That is so dumb and pointless. This is never going to work! I'm leaving." I do my best to turn the wheelchair around, but it's a bit difficult at first. Suddenly, I'm off and heading back to my room.

I arrive at my room in the hospital and I find my mom there. A couple of my friends are there, too. Lauren and Sam are sitting by the window. They stare at me, and I wonder what to tell them.

"Hey, umm how are you?" I ask.

They still say nothing. I then realize that they don't know what to say, at least I hope so because if not this is pretty awkward.

"So, I guess you've heard the news about my legs."

Lauren replies, "Your mom called us, and we came as soon as we could. How are you feeling anyway?"

"I feel fine; I'm still the same. Except for the fact that I can't walk or do anything else with my legs!"

Sam asks, "Is there anything we can do for you? Just let us know."

"No, why would there be?" I reply harshly. Meanwhile, I was thinking the entire time about what I was going to do now, considering I can't walk or play basketball anymore. The realization that I'm mad at my friends makes me aware that it has nothing to do with them. I'm just maddened that all this happened. Now I have to somehow figure out what to do.

"Thanks for coming. I appreciate your concern for me, but I think I'm okay. Bye for now. We'll talk soon."

My friends leave and I decide that I may as well go to bed. Maybe I'll have a dream that will tell me what to do. At least, I hope so, because right now I've got nothing. Plus, I don't even know where to start.

"Breakfast the next morning is absolutely revolting, cold runny eggs, soggy oatmeal, semi-raw bacon and sour grapefruit juice."

Enough of that. Time to go see Lola again. I wheel myself out of my room and head down the hallway to her room, which already has people in it. They're doing crafts. They seem pretty happy considering they're in a hospital. I look around for Lola and notice that she's just finishing up talking to another patient, so I wave her over. As she gets closer she smiles and says, "I didn't expect to see you here, but I'm happy that you are."

"Yeah, well, I'm here. I decided that I still want to be the determined person that I've always been. In the past, I persevered through everything, but this obstacle has got me stuck. Even though I can't walk, I still want to be athletic somehow."

"I see your concern," replied Lola. "I have an idea, but I need more time to get all the facts. How about you come back here tomorrow morning at 9:00 a.m.?"

"Okay, I'll see you then. Bye."

As I wheel myself back to my room, I see a little boy in a wheelchair too. He's much younger than I am, but he looks very happy and cheerful. Maybe I could learn something from him? Perhaps I was put into a wheelchair for a reason? I should get back to my room; mom is probably wondering where I am.

My dinner is waiting for me. I guess I was gone longer than I thought. Time flies when you're having fun right…? NOT! Anyway, I finish eating and the nurses are making me go to bed, even though it's only 7:00 p.m. I hate the hospital!

Waking up the next morning, I realize how tired I am, but I'm still going to go see Lola. I'm really starting to get a handle on this "wheeling" myself around stuff. Anyway, I'm heading down to see Lola now, and I've got to say that I'm a bit nervous. I'm also curious about what Lola's "idea" is. Guess I'll find out now because I'm here.

"Hello, Reese. How are you today?" asks Lola.

"I'm alive, aren't I?"

"Okay, well I hope you'll feel better after hearing this news. I did a little research yesterday. I found multiple wheelchair basketball leagues right here in Hamilton."

"Really? There's such a thing as wheelchair basketball!?"

"Yes, there is. I thought you might like it."

I wondered how I would feel wheeling around the court instead of running.

"It's not going to be the same as regular basketball; it's going to be completely different."

"You won't know until you try it. In fact, many wheelchair athletes play in the Olympics."

"Really? Hmm, I guess I could give it a try. When can I start?" Suddenly, I begin to think that I could still have a life that involves basketball. It might even do some good.

"There's a game next week and they'd be happy to have you come. What do you say?"

"Sure. I'll go. It may not be the same as regular basketball, but at least I can still do what I love to the best of my ability."

"For sure, Reese, for sure. Always remember, that change is constant, and that sometimes… change is a good thing."

www.ingramcontent.com/pod-product-compliance
Ingram Content Group UK Ltd.
Pitfield, Milton Keynes, MK11 3LW, UK
UKHW041957230426
12048UKWH00008B/394